To Ch

All the Best

Kevin

Tintonia

Land of the Elfins

by

Kevin Gritten

authorHOUSE®

AuthorHouse™ UK Ltd.
500 Avebury Boulevard
Central Milton Keynes, MK9 2BE
www.authorhouse.co.uk
Phone: 08001974150

This book is a work of fiction. People, places, events, and situations are the product of the author's imagination. Any resemblance to actual persons, living or dead, or historical events, is purely coincidental.

© 2007 Kevin Gritten. All rights reserved.

No part of this book may be reproduced, stored in a retrieval system, or transmitted by any means without the written permission of the author.

First published by AuthorHouse 11/20/2007

ISBN: 978-1-4343-3208-0 (sc)

Printed in the United States of America
Bloomington, Indiana

This book is printed on acid-free paper.

This book was written for and is dedicated to Sam, Tom, Georgie and Becca.

I would like to thank my wife. Without her support, enthusiasm and editorial skills this book would not exist. My agent Darin Jewell for believing in Tintonia. To all the children who read Tintonia before publication giving me favourable reviews and encouragement. To Chloe Gritten for not putting the book down until she had finished. Most of all thanks to Samuel, Thomas, Georgina and Rebecca for just being our children. I love you all.

Chapter One

Into The Tunnels

A glorious sun shone down on the Kent countryside, warming the grass and sparkling on the water of a lake. Beside the lake stood two boys and two girls called Samuel, Thomas, Georgie and Rebecca. The two boys were eleven and the two girls nine, not two sets of twins, but brothers and sisters. Samuel and Georgie's father, Kevin lives with Thomas and Rebecca's mother, Jane in a large barn conversion in the heart of Kent in South East England. They all have their ups and downs and moans and groans, but, in general, they get on well and the bonds they have formed together will last them long and serve them well.

Kevin Gritten

"I'm bored." said Sam [one of his favourite sayings].

"You wouldn't be if you hadn't broken the rope swing." said Georgie.

"Why did you try to swing upside down by your legs anyway?" asked Thomas.

"I thought it would be fun." replied Sam.

"I didn't even get a go." said Rebecca.

"Sorry Becks." said Sam, "You can have first go next time."

"What next time?" exclaimed Georgie. "We haven't got a swing now!"

"Sorry Becks." said Sam again and he gave her a little hug. "Here, see how far you can skim this stone. It's really shiny I found it earlier. I've been saving it."

"Thanks." said Rebecca and she gave it a really hard throw. The stone skimmed the water four times before it finally sank.

"Cor, did you see that?" said Sam. "The best today, Your the champion Becks!" Rebecca smiled and the others all cheered as they all ran off into the woods that edged the lake.

With mousy hair and handsome faces, the two boys were both about the same height and build, just above average for their years. Georgie, despite being one of the youngest, was the tallest; with long legs and blond hair.

Rebecca was small for her age, short and petite, with longish hair. Even though she was short, Rebecca was quick, especially through the woods, with its' overhanging branches and brambles. She was already some way ahead and feeling very pleased with herself, as she often lagged behind the others in physical things, because of her size. Georgie was close behind and the boys brought up the rear, pretending to sword fight with branches they had picked up off the ground. Rebecca could see that the trees ahead were thinning, but the ground was getting darker, despite the sun. She slowed and stopped at the edge of the darker patch of ground but Georgie, thinking she would be in the lead, sped past onto the dark patch and immediately disappeared under the ground. Georgie screamed and Rebecca screamed and the woods echoed with the girls' cries. When Samuel and Thomas got to Rebecca, she stopped them and pointed to the ground saying.

"Georgie fell in! She went under the ground!"

"Don't be daft! People don't just sink under the ground!" said Thomas.

"She did! I saw her on the dark bit that looks all burnt!"

"Oh yeah; we believe you, thousands wouldn't." Sam laughed, giving Thomas a wink. "Come on Becks, where's she hiding?"

"She's not! She fell into the ground!" protested Rebecca. Just then a faint sound came to their ears. It sounded like Georgie's voice.

"Did you hear that?" asked Thomas.

"Yes. It sounded like Georgie and it came from under the ground." said Sam. They all shouted Georgie's name and she replied.

"Come on down! It's wicked down here!" The other three just looked at each other in bewilderment "There's a big red cushion and the walls are bright pink!" Georgie giggled.

"She's hit her head." Sam said to Thomas. "But how are we going to get her back up?"

"I'm not coming up." came Georgie's voice from below. "You come down here!" Sam, Thomas and Rebecca looked at the ground and then at each other. Then Rebecca said "I'm not going on there. I thought it looked scary. That's why I stopped." Sam turned to her, looked at her with a caring look then said.

"Don't worry Becks. Don't be scared." Then he pushed her onto the dark patch and she disappeared beneath the ground. "Crikey!" he said. "It really works! That's well cool."

"Why did you do that?" shouted Thomas. "That's my sister you've pushed into God knows where."

"My sister's down there too, you know and anyway, someone had to test it." With that he jumped and also disappeared below the surface. Within seconds Thomas could hear laughter and giggling below the surface, then shouts from all three below.

"Come on Tom. Jump Get down here, it's so cool" he heard Sam say.

"There are lights and sparkles and everything!" Rebecca added Thomas looked around took a deep breath then stepped forward onto the dark ground. His feet went through the earth, and before he new it, he was falling. He wasn't scratched or bumped by roots and stones as he had expected but floated down, slowly, without effort or pain. He fell in darkness, but wasn't afraid because everything around him was calm and warm. Then he popped out into bright light and fell fast, like a bird in a steep dive. He landed on a large red cushion and bounced for a while until the momentum stopped. He crawled off the cushion and found Sam, Georgie and Rebecca standing in front of him.

"There. Told you! Wasn't that just the coolest thing you've ever done?" said Sam.

"I want to do it again." said Rebecca excitedly.

"We will have to get back up first and we can't do that from here." said Georgie. The room was quite large and painted pink, just like Georgie had said. The only item in the room was the large red cushion and the light seemed to seep from the walls, as there were no lights to speak of.

"How do we get out of here?" asked Thomas,

"We go this way." answered Sam. He had wandered off into a corner of the room and had found a tunnel. As he walked into it, light came from the walls. The further he walked, the more light appeared.

"It must be some sort of phosphorous generating the lights and it must be operated by sensors" said Thomas, whom it must be said is a bit of a bright spark himself.

"What's posporous?" asked Rebecca, who sometimes had her own unique way of talking.

"He means the walls shine and they come on as you walk through." answered Georgie. "Don't worry, he's just showing off. Come on, follow me!" She walked into the tunnel and passed Sam.

"Hey!" protested Sam. "I was in the lead! Come on Becks. I'll look after you."

"You?" she said

"You pushed me down here."

"Just think of the fun you're going to have." Sam replied. He took her by the hand and they followed Georgie.

"Oh, just leave me 'til last again! Don't ask my opinion. I might not want to go!" said Thomas. He thought about this then ran after the others. They walked on with the lights coming on in front of them and then going off behind them as they made their way along the tunnel. They passed two other passages but decided to carry on in a straight line, owing to the smells and the noises coming from the other directions.

"Mummy and Kevin are going to be worried if we don't get home soon." said Rebecca.

"Well we can't do anything about that now." said Thomas. "We will just have to explain when we get home."

"I bet we get sent to bed early." groaned Sam.

"Look!" shouted Georgie with excitement. "The tunnel's getting brighter and larger. I'm sure we're nearly at the end!" They all ran. Georgie was right. They came out of the tunnel and into the open air. Blue skies and white clouds were above them and they could feel a breeze and hear running water. As they ran out they noticed that the ground was covered with bones! Hundreds and thousands of bones!

Chapter Two

The Bone Giant

They walked out into the field and looked around. The air was warm and it could have been a bright summers day, in the school holidays, if it wasn't for all the bones around them. They weren't just lying on the ground but stacked in neat little piles , very close together with paths between them. All the piles had labels on them and Thomas read some. A large pile was labelled "Fire Breathing Dragon" another, said "A Knight Of The Round Table" and another, "My Brother Dennis". They all looked at each other in complete amazement when Thomas read that one.

"I need a wee" said Sam.

"Go in the Knights helmet" said Georgie.

"I can't do that, can I?" asked Sam.

"Well there's no where else" said Georgie. Sam was by now jumping up and down from one leg to the other, holding his hands between his legs. The other three were watching him giggling away when they all jumped with surprise as a loud voice behind them said "Who are you and what do you think you are doing in my bone collection?" They all turned to see the most frightening sight. There stood a Giant. He must have been at least eleven feet tall with big feet in bright red boots. He had shaggy brown hair and was dressed in black leather, like he had just got off a motorbike but the worst thing was that he only had one eye, big and blue and bloodshot, right in the middle of his enormous head.

"I think I need to wee too" whimpered Rebecca.

"Come on! Answer!" growled the Giant.

"We didn't know it was your bone collection" replied Thomas politely. "We just wandered out here through that tunnel."

"Oh." Said the giant "From the world above are you?"

"Yes," said Georgie, "Can you tell us how to get back?" She was a little frightened and it showed in her voice.

"Well you can't get back that way." He said, "You can only get in." "How do you think some of these bones got here?"

"I'm more worried about what happened after they got here" replied Georgie.

"Well," said the Giant "Some were stewed, some were boiled and some roasted. That's my favourite with vegetables and gravy." He was leaning over now, his head getting closer to the children. "Then I clean the bones, put them in piles and label them." "So, what are your names so I have something to put on the labels?"

"I don't like this Giant," said Rebecca "He's big and horrid and smelly. I want to go home Thomas! I want to go home!" The Giant laughed and Thomas put his arms around Rebecca. Then a sound came to their ears, a tinkling sound like running water. Thomas, Georgie and Rebecca turned and the Giant stopped laughing to followed their stares. Sam, unable to hold on any longer, had weed in the knight's helmet. He turned to see everyone looking at him as he zipped himself up.

"What?" he said. "I really needed that. Now what were you saying? Something about not getting back that way?" The Giant exploded into an enormous roar.

"You weed on my bones you filthy boy. You're not fit for sausages. I'll eat you all and I'll start with you!" He reached down and grabbed Georgie by the left leg and held her upside down in the air. Georgie screamed and screamed with all her might.

"Put my sister down!" shouted Sam.

"Georgie!" yelled Thomas and Rebecca just covered her eyes with her hands. Now you might not know this but Giants, especially ones with only one eye, have very sensitive hearing and Georgie's screams were more than this Giant could bear.

"Stop that noise!" he shouted, putting his free hand over one ear. "You're hurting my ears you stupid girl!" Rebecca took her hands away from her eyes, looked at the scene and sensing that this would give them all a bit more time shouted.

"Keep screaming Georgie!" Sam turned to Thomas and said,

"I know how he feels. Her screams go right through my head too. It hurts my ears! Does she really have to keep that up Rebecca?"

"Stop thinking of yourself Sam and do something!" she replied. Sam and Thomas looked at each other, then looked around. Sam picked up a skull and threw it to Thomas.

"Catch!" he said. He then picked up a long bone and held it in his hand like a club. "Come on Thomas bowl it to me." Thomas, catching on, bowled the skull underarm and Sam hit it first time at the Giant's head. It hit him in his eye and he immediately let go of Georgie to cover the eye with his hand. Georgie fell to the ground and ended up sitting down, still screaming.

"Don't stop screaming!" said Thomas. So Georgie carried on and the Giant stamped his feet and roared,

"Stop it! Stop it!"

"Run Rebecca." said Thomas. "We'll follow."

Rebecca did not need any encouragement. She turned on her heels and ran as fast as she could. When she was some fifty feet away she hid behind a large pile of bones labelled *The Three Little Pigs*. This puzzled Rebecca as she was sure that The Three Little Pigs were chased by a wolf, not a Giant.

Anyway they weren't eaten. She shook this thought from her mind and looked over the top of the pile. Georgie was still on the ground screaming and Sam and Thomas were jumping and diving out of the way of the Giants fists as he thumped the ground around them.

"Squash you! Squash you! Suck your bones clean!" roared the giant. Sam ducked to his right under a Giant hand, scrambled forward and tripped over a pile of bones labelled *'Roman Gladiator'*.

Thomas was by now on his back, having fallen over a bone from one of the other piles. He was pushing himself away, using his hands and feet, in a frantic attempt to keep away from the Giant's blows.

At this moment Sam jumped up from behind the pile he had just fallen over.

"Yeah, Ha!" he shouted "Look at me Georgie!" Sam was wearing a bronze helmet with a red plume, a small bronze shield on one arm and he was holding a gleaming Roman short sword in his hand. Georgie stopped screaming and shouted at Sam.

"Stop messing around and help Thomas! The Giant has almost got him!" Then she continued to scream to keep the Giant confused. The Giant was by now on his hands and knees, his head spinning with the sound of Georgies' screams. He was following Thomas purely by smell, lashing out with his huge fists, trying to hit him but just knocking over piles and piles of bones.

"I'll get you for ruining my bone collection!" Sam had, by now, rushed up behind the Giant and with a huge effort he plunged the sword into the Giant's bottom. The Giant let out a hideous wail and swung his arm around behind him. Sam raised his shield and this took the force of the blow but it sent Sam flying into a large pile of bones with a label that read *Two Nuns and a Priest*. Realising he had a chance to escape, Thomas got to his feet and ran in Rebecca's direction. Georgie stopped screaming got up and ran over to where Sam had just landed.

"Did you see that?" Sam said, a bit dazed and confused. Georgie had a job getting him to his feet. "He had green sparkly blood!"

"Yes I know." Said Georgie "You've got it all down your front. Dad's going to kill you, if the Giant doesn't first! Come on! Let's run! He's trying to pull the sword out!" They got to their feet and ran for their lives, ignoring the moans and curses coming from the Giant behind them. They reached Thomas and Rebecca and then they all ran off together, trying to put as much ground as possible between them and the Giant. They heard a loud roar, something flying through the air and a crash behind them. As they ran they looked over their shoulders to see that the Giant had taken the sword from his bottom and had thrown it after them. It had landed on the pile of bones that Rebecca had been hiding behind.

"That was a close call!" shouted Sam.

"I'm not sure if you're a hero or a complete twit!" said Thomas you've made him twice as angry and now he's chasing us!"

"Stop chatting and run!" said Georgie.

"Yes let's get out of here." said Rebecca. They ran and ran, with what looked like high cliffs on either side of them in the distance, straight ahead seemed the only way to go. The ground was still flat and still covered with piles of bones, which they ran in and out of. The Giant, could step over all of the piles but his progress was limited because of his wound and he was limping badly. The children were tiring by now and Rebecca, who was in front, shouted "I can't go on like this! I can't run anymore!"

"You've got to! We've got to keep going!" urged Georgie.

"I think we'll have to stop and fight." said Sam. "See if you can find another Roman gladiator or Knight of the Round Table"

"Don't be silly!" said Thomas. "You were lucky last time. We've got to keep going." Just then Rebecca stopped in her tracks and let out a huge despairing sigh.

"Oh no," she groaned. The ground in front of them where Rebecca now stood had disappeared and had fallen away down a sheer drop.

They couldn't tell how deep the drop was but it was rocky and misty at the bottom. Ahead of them grass covered the other side with no bones in sight but the gap was too wide for them to jump.

"There must be a way to cross" said Georgie, looking from side to side.

"I don't think so." said Thomas. "The grass is clear over there with no bones so obviously the Giant can't get across. If he can't, neither can we!"

"Can we climb down?" asked Rebecca.

"It's too steep." answered Thomas.

"Well what are we going to do?" panicked Georgie.

"Fight!" roared Sam with excitement.

He was by now shuffling through piles of bones, looking for weapons but could find none. Eventually he came over to the others with the news.

"Sorry. No swords, axes, clubs or anything, so fighting's out of the question."

"Perhaps we could get Georgie to scream again?" suggested Rebecca.

"I can't keep that up all day and anyway it doesn't stop him from trying to squash us."

"Shut up the lot of you!" barked Thomas. He was now peering over the edge of the cliff, studying the scene below. "I'm sure that what we're looking at is not real." He said. "The edges are wavy and the whole thing keeps moving and every now and then it flashes really quickly. See! It did it then!"

"Oh yes, so it does. Very pretty," agreed Georgie. "But what does it mean?"

"I think," said Thomas "that it's a kind of mirage we're seeing but it's not really there."

"That's all very interesting but that Giant's almost here and we have nowhere to go" said Sam.

"But that's the point." Said Thomas infuriated by the other's lack of understanding. "I think it's like the grass before, It's not real. Perhaps there's another cushion down there."

"Oh goody!" beamed Rebecca. "I liked that cushion." The Giant was by now almost upon them and he was picking up bones and throwing them, while the children dodged them.

"O.K." said Sam. "All join hands."

"Why?" asked Rebecca.

"It's time we put Thomas' idea to the test." They all joined hands because no one wanted to jump alone.

"Right 1, 2, 3, go!" shouted Sam and they all jumped. Just in time to as the Giant had just reached them. He growled and roared at the top of his voice.

"You silly kids, jumping to your deaths! What a waste of bones!"

Chapter Three

The Bay

The children didn't hear the Giants words as they fell. They were too busy worrying about the fall and about what would happen when they finally hit the bottom. As it happened they need not have worried. Thomas had been dead right about the picture that they could see from above. It was exactly that. A Picture, a mirage, call it what you like. They glided down and landed on another huge cushion, a blue one this time. They bounced around and then they all fell off into a heap.

"I love these cushions." said Rebecca, "That's my favourite bit of this adventure so far." The room they were in was similar to the one they had fallen into before, except the cushion was blue and the walls brown, instead of bright pink. The light was just the same and they soon found a tunnel, like the one before. They started to make their way through it. After a while they came to the end and walked out again into bright sunshine.

"I hope there are NO giants this time!" said Rebecca.

"Me too!" said Sam. "I'm too tired for all that again!" All four of them were dirty and worn out from their adventure so far. As they walked into the sunshine, they saw a most beautiful sight. They had walked out onto a sandy beach; a bay; just like the ones the children had seen on holiday in Cornwall. On the cliff there were the ruins of a castle, like the one at Tintagel where King Arthur was supposed to have had his round table and where Lancelot and Guinervere fell in love. There were rock pools and waves breaking on the beach. The children stopped and took in the view then ran, yelling and laughing, to the water's edge. Rebecca said "Let's get out of these dirty clothes, wash them and dry them on the rocks!"

"Good idea." said Georgie. "Sam's all covered in Giant's blood." They all looked at Sam. He was standing looking at himself. He was the messiest of the four, which was usually the case but today he was worse than usual.

Kevin Gritten

"O.K." he said "Let's get on with it." Thomas looked at the water and said

"Hold on. We don't know what could be in that water. This place is full of surprises."

"We need to wash and I'm all hot and bothered." said Georgie.

"Yes and the water looks so good." Said Rebecca. So, giggling and laughing again, the children got undressed down to their underwear and they jumped into the water. They washed their clothes and themselves, put their clothes on the rocks to dry and then the boys lay in the sun to dry, whilst the girls played in the water. They were splashing each other when another face appeared between them, popping up out of the water.

"Hello, I'm Narda. Who are you?" It was a girl's face but it gave Rebecca and Georgie a bit of a fright. They thought at first that it was one of the boys, playing a trick until they realised this new face belonged to another girl. Rebecca and Georgie looked at each other and then Rebecca answered.

"I'm Rebecca and this is Georgie. The two boys on the beach are called Sam and Thomas; our brothers. "Are you a wermaid?" she asked Narda.

"Yes." Was the reply and Narda dived under the water and they saw her tail breach the surface. Then Narda circled underwater before appearing between them again. Whilst Narda was underwater, Georgie said

"It's mermaid, not wermaid Rebecca."

"I know what I mean," replied Rebecca. "And I like wermaid." As I have said before, Rebecca has her own way with words sometimes. "Sam! Thomas! Look. A wermaid!" shouted Rebecca.

"Mermaid!" hissed Georgie. The boys looked up and saw Narda.

"Just great!" said Sam. "We find someone friendly and it's another girl. "What's a wermaid anyway?"

"She means mermaid." said Thomas.

"Oh." said Sam and they lay down again. Rebecca looked at the mermaid and thought how lovely she looked In fact she reminded Rebecca of her elder sister, Victoria and for a moment her mind wandered off. She wondered if she would ever see Victoria or her niece, Chloe again.

"Can you tell us how to get out of here?" asked Georgie.

"Where did you come from?" asked Narda.

"From up there." answered Rebecca.

"Oh," said Narda "from the world above. Well you can't go back that way and I wouldn't try to cross this sea. The dangers are too great."

"Well, where should we go next?" asked Georgie.

Kevin Gritten

"All I know is that there are three tunnels leading from this bay; two right and one left. I know not where they lead or if the destinations are good or bad but you will have to make a choice, one word of advice however. The easy route is not always the best one and sometimes you may have to go down before going up." The boys were pondering the question about which way to go next.

"Three tunnels." said Thomas. "How do we work out which way to go, I wonder?"

"Easy" said Sam. He stood and pointed at each tunnel in turn. Starting with the one on the left and speaking in rhyme said, "Eanie, Meanie, Miney, Mo which way should we go? Be it easy or be it tough, we'll just have to take pot luck." His rhyme stopped as he pointed to the tunnel at the top right hand side of the bay. "That way" said Sam "It's as good as any."

"I think we can be a little more scientific than that." said Thomas.

"How?" asked Sam.

"Well let's go and look at the entrances to the tunnels to see if they go up or down. We need to go up so if one does that , then we will take that one." Said Thomas trying to convince himself as well as Sam.

"And what if more than one goes up or none of them do?" asked Sam.

"Then we go with Eanie, Meanie, Miney, Mo. O.K?" said Thomas.

"O.K." agreed Sam. So, dressed in clean dry clothes they wandered off to explore.

Meanwhile, the girls were still playing with Narda.

"My ankle and leg really hurts, from where that Giant grabbed me" said Georgie. "I think I may have a bruise."

"Here let me help." said Narda enthusiastically and she swam under the water and touched Georgie's leg. Immediately her leg and ankle felt warm and the pain subsided. Narda surfaced again and smiled.

"There how is that?" she asked.

"It feels fine." said Georgie. "All of the pain has gone and I feel great."

"How did you do that?" asked Rebecca.

"Didn't you know that mermaids can heal?" said Narda. "How do you think we save ship-wreaked sailors and how do you think we nurse the whales and the dolphins? We have magical healing powers. We can give others part of our life's energy so that they can live on. That's our purpose in life; to help others. You have never heard of a bad mermaid have you?" Narda finished. Rebecca had to admit she hadn't and that this all made perfect sense to her. So she said

"No." and asked "Can you bring people back to life if they die?"

"I am afraid not" was the answer "We can only help those near to death or in need of a little help, like Georgie was."

"Do it for me!" Rebecca insisted very excited.

"But you're not unwell." replied Narda.

"Oh yes, I didn't think of that." said Rebecca.

"However I will give you a gift to carry with you." said Narda and she touched Rebecca with her finger; in the middle of Rebecca's head. At once Rebecca felt a warm glow on her skin and her body seemed to surge with energy. It made her feel faint for a second but then she just felt so alive.

"There, now you can heal." said Narda. She was looking very tired now and her face looked grey and unwell. "I have given you all the energy that I can without harming myself. If any of you fall ill or get hurt, just touch that person and they will recover but be sparing with this gift, because in a human it will not last long." Narda then dived under the water and swam off to rest until she was strong again.

"Wow Rebecca! Did you hear that? She gave you some of her healing powers!"

"Yes Georgie, I know but I wish she could have stayed longer. Let's go and get dressed." So they dried themselves in the sun and dressed in the washed clothes and lay on the beach until the boys returned from their walk. As the boys walked back to where the girls lay on the sand, they talked.

"So, we go with the tunnel I suggested, yeah?" said Sam.

"O. K." replied Thomas. "Seeing as how all of them seem as flat each other, One tunnel is as good as another. Let's talk to the girls." They all chatted together for about half an hour. The boys told how they had explored all the tunnels and that they all seemed the same so they had decided to chose one by chance. The girls told the boys all about Narda and how she had healed Georgie's foot and had given Rebecca the gift of healing. They all lay down beside each other and tiredness overcame them.

They fell into a deep sleep and started to dream. Sam dreamed of dragons and swords, fast cars and home. He missed home. Thomas dreamed of books, school, football and home. He missed home. Georgie dreamed of princess and horses, Cinderella and home. She missed home. Rebecca dreamed of Barbies, Brides and flowers and she too dreamed of home. She missed home. They all missed home, their parents, friends and the security they all felt at home.

Chapter Four

Bad Fairies

When they awoke they all felt refreshed and ready to go on. They had no idea how long they had slept but guessed it must have been for quite a long time. They were all very hungry and decided that wherever they ended up, food would be a priority. They tried the tunnel chosen by Sam, which was short but this led to a swamp grey and cold and horrible and even though Narda had said that the easy route would not always be the best route, they all decided to go back and start again. Sam went through his Eanie, Meanie routine again; this time with only two tunnels and they headed down the second tunnel on the right. This was longer and became very small so that towards the end they had to crawl on all fours to eventually climb out.

They emerged into a forest of thick vegetation, tall trees and bracken, with moss underfoot and trickling streams. Animal sounds broke the silence, mainly birds but others that the children couldn't identify. They surveyed the dense woodland but could see no obvious path to follow.

"Which way?" asked Georgie.

"I've no idea." answered Thomas.

"Well, we can't stay here," said Sam "so let's go this way. The trees seem a little thinner."

"It's colder here" remarked Rebecca.

"The sun can't get through the trees." said Thomas. They walked on in silence for a while, Sam in the lead, then Rebecca, then Georgie and finally Thomas bringing up the rear so that neither of the girls would be left behind or feel scared. Silly really, because both the boys felt as scared as the girls. This place was spooky and none of them really wanted to be there. Worse than that though were the noises, gradually all of them became aware of something following them. It would be on one side then it would drop back, cross over and appear on the other side or run off in front, cross over and appear again. They could see nothing, except a few bushes, moving or bits of bracken and undergrowth but they could hear it and it sounded horrid. Sick with fright, tiredness and hunger the children struggled on through the thickening vegetation until the light began to fail. Then they stood on a slightly thinner piece of ground where two trees had fallen.

"This is as good a place as any." said Sam.

"We can't stop now." said Thomas with a sense of urgency in his voice.

"Well, we can't go on." replied Sam. "We're all too tired and anyway we're lost, with no idea of where we're going." Thomas looked at Sam and knew he was right. He looked at the two girls, huddled together against one of the fallen trees; silent; their eyes full of dread, thinking about what might come out of the dark.

"O.K." said Thomas "what's the plan?"

"No plan," said Sam. "Just pick up one of the broken branches, stand in front of the girls and if anything comes near us, we hit it as hard as we can."

"I'm not sure I've got the strength." said Thomas.

"Me neither," replied Sam. "But what else can we do?" Both boys were still looking at Georgie and Rebecca, whose expressions and position had not changed. It was as if they had heard nothing of the boy's conversation but had just been looking into the gloom; listening for whatever had been following them.

"I can't hear it anymore." Georgie whispered, as much to herself as anyone else.

"Perhaps it's gone." said Rebecca, more in hope than conviction. So with the two boys standing guard, in turns, the girls tried to sleep; but sleep would not come and the forest became even darker. After maybe one or two hours with Thomas on guard and Sam trying to reassure the girls that things could only get better, strange buzzing sounds started to break the silence of the forest; different to the sounds that had followed them earlier. No these came from the air above them, then lights, small and dim but lights all the same. They floated down from the canopy above, buzzing and crackling as they came and yes, the lights appeared to be laughing! Sam and the girls stood next to Thomas and Sam asked

"Can you hear that? Those lights are laughing!"

"Yes," replied Thomas "and I think I can see shapes in the lights."

"They're fairies!" shouted Rebecca. Her spirits lifted by these small figures that glowed in the dark.

"You're right." said Georgie. "They're easier to see now that they are closer." They held out their hands and the fairies danced around them. The children watched and completely forgot about the other sounds they had heard and about all their troubles. The girls jumped up and down and felt happier than they had since leaving the cove and the mermaid, Narda.

Then things changed. The fairies started to buzz louder and fly faster. They dive-bombed the children and pinched them and pulled their hair, and threw small stones and twigs. More and more of them joined in and Georgie and Rebecca ended up huddled under one of the fallen trees again, while the boys flailed at the air with sticks but the fairies were to quick. Things were getting out of hand and the boys were just about to suggest running again when a low growl echoed around the children. The fairies stopped and hovered in mid-air, looking towards the other fallen tree. Thomas and Sam followed their gaze and Georgie and Rebecca came out from under their tree. They all stared, along with the fairies, at the figure before them.

"Should we run now?" suggested Georgie, in a whisper to Thomas.

"I think we should wait. These fairies seem to be afraid of this creature." Thomas whispered back. The figure before them was short and squat with long arms and short legs which made him look ape-like. It held onto the tree with huge feet and long toes which had talons that gripped the bark. It's skin was green, pimpled with odd black spots. This new sight was dressed in dark cloth trousers and top with a tight, fitting cap of the same material which fitted around his large, green, pointed ears. It wore a black leather belt with a knife attached to it and carried a black leather bag over one shoulder and a whip in one hand. So there they all were, sizing each other up; the children and this new creature.

After what seemed like an age, but was probably only minutes, the fairies decided that this new creature was no threat and they turned their attention back to the children. The boys had anticipated this and had already told the girls to take cover again. As the fairies prepared to attack once more they swung out with their makeshift weapons. Both Sam and Thomas hit their targets and sent fairies flying under their blows but, after this the remainder were up to speed and once again too quick. Sam received a bite on the back of one hand. At this point the creature on the fallen tree began to react. He used his whip to hit the fairies. As quick as they were, he was quicker and sent them flying in all directions.

Very soon the fairies had had enough and they disappeared, taking any fallen comrades with them.

"Thanks." Thomas said to the creature.

"Gordo." replied the creature. "Gordo's the name. Been following you, I have. Knew you'd 'ave fairy trouble coming this way." His voice was gruff and he kept his words short, as if saving breath.

"I thought fairies were supposed to be good." Said Rebecca.

"Not all." replied Gordo. "Some's bad especially along here."

"What or who are you?" asked Georgie.

"Gordo" came the reply. "That's who I am. As for what I am, I'm a forest goblin. A forest goblin that's how I knows how to deal with bad fairies." At that moment Sam groaned and complained about the bite on his hand. Then he fell, flat on his face, into a puddle.

"Oh no!" shouted Georgie. "What's wrong with him?"

"Fairy bite" replied Gordo. "Poison in the blood. We'll have to bleed him. There are plants that can help if I can find some but it's very dark". He looked around whilst still perched on the fallen tree.

"No, wait! Let me!" cried Rebecca. Stepping forward she turned Sam over with Tom's help, found the bite on Sam's hand and touched it lightly with her finger. She closed her eyes and thought of Narda. At once she felt a warm glow and felt a surge like a transfer of power go from her to Sam. He sat up with a start, coughing and spluttering, took Rebecca in his arms and gave her a hug.

"Thanks, Becks" he said. "I was nearly gone. You saved my life." Thomas and Georgie smiled but Gordo looked amazed. As Georgie and Rebecca helped Sam to his feet, Thomas went to chat to Gordo.

"Can you help us some more?" he asked. "We're wet, tired and hungry and it looks like Sam needs to rest for a while before we can continue with our journey."

"Food, a place to stay, somewhere to sleep, safe from bad fairies?" Gordo replied "Oh yes, I can help with that but what I want to know is how did she do that? I thought your friend was a gonna." he said with a hint of disbelief in his voice.

"She's a healer" said Georgie. "A mermaid called Narda gave her the power. It won't last forever but she said it would be useful."

"A mermaid!" exclaimed Gordo "Gave her power! Well, I never heard of such a thing. I shall take you to the nearest village. You can eat and get some rest and maybe you can do someone a favour in return before you continue on your journey. By the way, where are you going?" asked Gordo.

"Back home to our world" said Sam, who was by now on his feet, brushing himself off. Once again he was the dirtiest of them all.

"The world above, we've heard it called" remarked Thomas.

"Oh, the world above?" repeated Gordo. "So you're humans?"

"Yes" said Georgie, "Human children."

"Haven't seen many human children before" answered Gordo. "I had forgotten you were so ugly." This remark made the children giggle at each other as Gordo resembled nothing more than a Warthog. If they were ugly, what was he? Anyway, once Gordo had jumped down from his perch and had started to make his way through the forest, the children fell in behind him and fell silent, hoping that the village wasn't too far. After a short distance, Gordo stopped and pointed to a tall tree.

"We go up here" said Gordo, taking hold of a rope ladder on the far side of the tree.

"I don't want to go up there" said Rebecca.

"We have to" urged Georgie. "We have to follow Gordo if we want to get out of this place."

"Come on Becks. I'll climb up behind you and I will help if you need me" encouraged Sam. The tree was very tall and the climb treacherous as the rope ladder swung from side to side but all of the children made it to the top. They had to climb off onto a sort of platform, in the canopy of the tree. It had a rail made of rope and wood, going all the way around it and the children were glad of the support.

"That was a heck of a climb" stuttered Thomas feeling very uneasy on his feet.

"Sure was" agreed Sam.

"Where do we go now, Gordo?" asked Georgie.

"Into the basket on the other side" Gordo answered. They all walked around the trunk of the tree and found a large wicker basket hanging above them. Gordo put up a hand and grabbed a handle on the bottom of the basket. Pulling it down, he attached it to the trunk by a hook and then told the children to climb in. Once they had all climbed in, Gordo followed.

"What happens now?" asked Rebecca. She had not liked the climb or being on the platform, so high up. Just like her mum, she did not like heights at all and now she was sitting in a basket, high above the ground, attached to a tree by nothing more than what looked like home made rope.

"This is what happens now" answered Gordo and he knocked off the hook that was holding the basket. The basket immediately sprang into the air and shot out over the rail, still supported by the rope. All the children held on for grim death. Rebecca screamed, Georgie closed her eyes and screamed, Sam yelled at the top of his voice and Thomas had his mouth open but was so scared that no sound came out of it. They shot in and out of the trees, rushing past other trees with platforms in them. At these points Gordo would pull or twist controlling levers which reached up to the rope that the basket traveled along. The levers helped to slow the basket and re-direct it. All four children started to get used to this way of travel. They could tell, by the way Gordo moved the levers, which way they would go next.

"This is wicked, once you get used to it! Isn't it?" said Thomas.

"Yeah," replied Sam "but you should have seen your face just now." They both laughed and watched the trees rush past.

"Are you O.K. Rebecca?" asked Georgie.

"Yes, I'm O.K. now" Rebecca answered.

"Will it be long, Gordo?" Georgie asked him.

"Not long" he replied "A few more trees." Sam and the others kept count of the trees in their heads. One, two, three, four, five. Then they slowly bumped into the trunk of the sixth tree, slid down and Gordo hooked the basket.

"That was the best ride I've ever been on." said Sam excitedly.

"I bet Kevin would like that" said Rebecca.

"You're right, Becks Dads just a big kid at heart." Georgie laughed.

"Come on," said Thomas. "Gordo's already climbing down the ladder!" The children followed Gordo and when they were at the bottom, Gordo led them off again, through the forest. After a short while, the trees thinned and they walked out into the open. Below they could see a valley full of lights from a town or village and their hearts lifted as they thought of food, beds and safety.

"Come on," urged Sam "let's run!"

"No!" shouted Gordo. "The pathways are not safe at this time of day."

"But it's starting to get light now" wined Georgie.

"Don't argue with Gordo" said Rebecca.

"So where do we go now?" asked Thomas.

"To my cabin" answered Gordo. "This way." He led them off to the right, along a ridge, into a glade and down a rocky path. They came to a large, log cabin with lights at the window. Gordo pushed open the door and shouted, "Mrs Gordo! Where are you? We have visitors!" They all filed into the cabin and watched as Mrs Gordo came out of a back room. She looked and was dressed very much like Gordo except that her clothes were more coloured and better kept. She also had a softer kinder look on her face and in her eyes.

"Oh my!" she was saying "Gordo, you're so late. I thought that the bad fairies had got you this time for sure."

"Never! I'm the best fairy masher ever!" replied Gordo.

"That's right" agreed Georgie. "He whipped them and saved us all."

"I used to like fairies but not anymore" added Rebecca.

"Not all fairies are bad. You just has to know which ones." Gordo said to the girls. "Mrs Gordo, meet my new friends, Thomas, Sam, Georgie and Rebecca. They're human children!"

"Human children? Oh my, whatever next?" exclaimed Mrs Gordo. "You poor dears. You must be very hungry. I've soup, bread and sausages with potatoes; all hot and ready so come and eat."

"Great!" Said Sam.

"Yes please!" said Thomas.

"Mmmm sausages, my favorite!" chirped Rebecca.

"I could eat a horse!" joked Georgie.

"Oh we don't eat horses here." said Gordo in a concerned voice and the others all looked at Georgie and smiled. Georgie just went red with embarrassment.

"Now sit at the table and Mrs Gordo will get your meal." They all ate well and while they ate they talked of home and told Gordo about their adventure so far. When everyone was full and all talked out, Mrs Gordo made up beds for them in the spare room. The children lay down and fell asleep, almost at once. Then they dreamed and wondered if anyone was missing them and when they would finally arrive home.

Chapter Five

The Elfins

In the morning, they all said goodbye to Mrs Gordo after a terrific breakfast of toast, eggs and cereal. Gordo led them back to the ridge, overlooking the valley with the village below them; just like the evening before. They could see golden fields of corn and rape below them and butterflies and bees swooped in and out of the wild flowers in the grass. It was a beautiful sight.

"What is that place called?" asked Rebecca.

"Tintonia." replied Gordo.

"Who lives there?" asked Georgie.

"The Elfins." said Gordo. "They may be able to help you to find your way home." he added. He walked off down a narrow, cobbled path and the children followed. They began to see why Gordo had not let them try the path at night. In places, the banks on either side of the path were very steep and rocks, thorn bushes and nettles were all very thick in these places. They crossed a bridge under which flowed lava, molten rock which spewed it's way out of the ground somewhere in the distance. Once they had come out of the side of the hills and into the valley they could run and play. This they did as Gordo trudged along the cobbled pathway.

As they drew closer to the village they began to see people, who stopped what they were doing to come and stare at them.

"Are they Elfins?" asked Thomas.

"Yes." replied Gordo. "And they are as curious about you as you are about them." More and more Elfins appeared as they drew closer to Tintonia as if a message had been sent ahead of them and people were coming to see what was happening. The Elfins were short in stature, not much bigger than Rebecca; even when fully grown so Georgie was taller than most grown-ups. They had thin faces, quite pale with bright green eyes, pointed ears like Gordo (although this was the only feature they shared) and small hands with only three fingers and a thumb on each hand. Most had long, straight hair but every now and then there was one with curly hair. Their clothes were mainly brown and grey, but highly decorated with bright coloured threads, in very beautiful patterns. Sam couldn't see any weapons, only farm tools and some (who looked like workmen) carried hammers and spades. They were just approaching the entrance to the village through a gate in a high fence that surrounded it when a familiar voice came to their ears from behind them

"Wait Gordo! Slow down!" It was Mrs Gordo, hurrying after them. "Oh, I'm so glad I caught up with you. I was so excited, thinking about you introducing our new friends to the Elfins, that I decided that I just had to come along."

"Good." said Gordo. "We can do some shopping whilst we're here Then we won't have to come back tomorrow." A young Elfin girl rushed up to Mrs Gordo and flung her arms around the goblin.

"Hello Mrs Gordo. How are you?" she said.

"Bless me!" exclaimed Mrs Gordo "If it isn't young Ramona! My, haven't you grown?" Some more children ran up to Mrs Gordo and it was obvious that they all knew her and liked her very much. "I've got some treats for you all." she continued and opened a small bag that she had brought with her. "Homemade sweets." she said. "Lime Tree Suckers, Mouse Tail Chews and your favourites, Stinging Nettle Jellies. The elfin children laughed and cheered and all jumped up and down trying to get to the front for their treats. "Here," said Mrs Gordo, holding the bag towards Sam, Thomas, Georgie and Rebecca "take some. There are plenty."

"Uggh! What's a Lime tree Sucker?" asked Sam.

"Oh, they're great!" replied Mrs Gordo and handed him one. The others watched as Sam touched it with his tongue then sucked the end and finally put the whole thing in his mouth, proclaiming

"Wow! It's terrific!" Rebecca chose a Mouse Tail Chew after Mrs Gordo assured her that it wasn't really made from the tails of mice. That was just a name. Georgie had a Stinging Nettle Jelly because it was red and it looked like a strawberry. Thomas also chose a Stinging Nettle Jelly.

"It takes forever to get all of the stings out." said Mrs Gordo. All four, plus Mrs Gordo were chatting and playing with the elfins when Mr Gordo broke up their play by saying.

"Come on, Mrs Gordo. We have to get these human children into the village as soon as possible."

"Oh, yes. Sorry." replied Mrs Gordo.

"Gordo, why do we need to get to the village so quickly?" asked Sam.

"There are people here who I want you to meet," Gordo replied "and I know that they are due to leave soon. I think you can help them or to be more precise, Rebecca can help them. In return they may find a way to get you back to the world above."

"How can I help?" asked Rebecca.

"Just be patient." he answered. They walked through the large gate in the fence, surrounding the village and Thomas wanted to know what the fence was there for."It's not always this peaceful here. Sometimes the dwarfs from the caverns, under Nightmare Mountain attack the village to steal cattle, horses and sheep and to take back prisoners to dig in the dwarf mines." Gordo explained.

"Would they try to take us prisoners?" asked Georgie.

"Oh, yes." answered Gordo. "You'd be a fine catch for the dwarfs." The children didn't like the sound of that and became very quiet, just thinking about it.

Once inside the gate, more adult Elfins came to see the new visitors. Gordo spoke to some and they pointed to a large building, some way off, in the centre of the village. Around them were what, looked like houses and barns and in one corner a church. The building they were now heading for looked like a kind of hall or meeting place. They walked up to the door, followed by what was now, quite a large crowd. Gordo entered, followed by the children and an Elfin that Gordo called Tig Tig. Tig Tig stopped everyone else from entering and the crowd stood outside. When Tig Tig closed the doors behind them, he turned to Gordo and asked

"Now, Gordo, tell me again. Who are these human children and why is it so important that you talk to Prince Rodric?" Gordo introduced the children, one by one, and then beckoned to Rebecca to come forward.

"These children have met the mermaid, Narda," Gordo announced "and she gave Rebecca the gift of healing. Now do you understand why it is so important that I speak to Prince Rodric?"

"How do you know she can really heal? She doesn't look particularly strong." commented Tig Tig.

"I've seen it wiv me own eyes." answered Gordo. "She healed Sam when he was bitten by a bad fairy, in the dark wood." Tig Tig fell silent at this revelation and regarded the children, staring into their eyes as if he could tell that what Gordo had said was a lie, just by looking at them.

"Wait here." Said Tig Tig and he turned and walked up some stairs and disappeared.

"Do you want me to heal someone?" asked Rebecca.

"All will become clear very soon, my dear." said Mrs Gordo.

"I'm getting worried about this," Sam whispered to Thomas. "We had better be prepared to run for it."

"Why?" asked Thomas. "Everyone seems very friendly." Still whispering, Sam continued,

"I don't like the way they won't tell us what they want Rebecca to do. For all we know, they might want to make soap out of her."

"Soap???" gasped Thomas. To which Mrs Gordo said, "Soap? Why, you only washed this morning."

"I know." said Sam. "I was just saying what lovely soap you have. What do you make it out of?" he asked.

"Berries and some petals from wild flowers and the oil from a special tree." she answered in a bemused manner. Then she turned to Georgie and asked, in a low voice, "Is he always this interested in soap?"

"Well," answered Georgie. "Let's just say he gets to use it more often than most." Sam was glaring at Thomas.

"Sorry." said Thomas. "Let's just keep our eyes open and if anything bad happens, we'll run. O.K?"

"Alright." said Sam.

"It's rude to whisper." said Georgie to the boys. "If you want soap that badly, I'm sure that Mrs Gordo will find you some."

"No. No, we're perfectly O.K." said Sam. Then Gordo spoke, sounding much more serious now,

"Quiet! All of you! I think Tig Tig's coming back." They all looked up the stairs and saw Tig Tig returning with two other people. The first was another Elfin, taller than most. He had a regal air about him, with a handsome face and much finer clothes than most of the other Elfins they had seen. They guessed that this must be Prince Rodric. The other person was older and even taller. He did not look like an Elfin at all and had a very hard, stern look upon his face. He had a completely bald head and no eyebrows. He was dressed in long, dark blue robes.

"This is Prince Rodric." Tig Tig announced. "And this is our wizard, Doctor Eric Von Hitzvelger."

"Hello and welcome to you all." said Prince Rodric. The children said hello to the prince and the doctor but the doctor said nothing.

"Will you all please come this way?" Tig Tig said and he led them into another room.

The room was light but spartan with only a huge table, surrounded by chairs. A few paintings hung on the walls but there was no carpet. Everyone sat around one end of the table with Prince Rodric at the head. The doctor sat to one side of him and Tig Tig, to the other.

"Before we start," said Thomas, "I want to ask something, please."

"Very well please continue." answered Prince Rodric. Everyone looked at Thomas and he felt very uncomfortable as he started to speak.

"Gordo has brought us here because he says we, or rather Rebecca can help you and that you can help us to reach home but he won't tell us what Rebecca can do to help you or how soon you can help us to return home. Rebecca thinks that you want her to heal someone. Is this right? Will you answer these questions for us?" Prince Rodric looked at Gordo, then at Tig Tig and finally at the doctor.

"Time for truth and openness I think." Rodric announced as he stood and walked around his chair. Standing behind it, he rested his hands on the back. "I am Lord here" he started. "I oversee this part of the Elfin lands. My brother does the same, for another village and lands south of here." He broke off for a moment and seemed to be thinking about how he should continue. "His wife has recently had a baby but has since fallen ill. You would not know but if an Elfin mother or child falls ill, within one year of being born, then the other would also fall ill. They are linked by a bond, which is only broken by the passing of one full year. If mother or child dies, the other will die also. My brother's wife and baby were sent here because the air is said to be better and Doctor Hitzvelger is our most famous wizard. Unfortunately, neither the air, nor the good doctor has been able to help and both baby and mother grow weaker by the day. The doctor's last hope was that we should take them both to see the mermaids and ask for their help. Gordo knew this and obviously, thought of us when he met you. As for getting you home, yes I think we can help you. My only questions to you are, have you really met the mermaid, Narda and if so, will Rebecca help us?" Prince Rodric stood behind his chair and the tears were visible in his eyes and the last of his words were very shaky and uncontrolled. Then Dr Hitzvelger spoke for the first time in a thickly Arian accent.

"If this human can heal, as Gordo says, ve should test her first." He said.

"No!" shouted Rebecca and she stood, banging her hands on the table. "Narda said that I should not waste the gift and it would not last long." Then she sat down again.

"Don't worry." said Georgie. "We all love you and we won't let anything happen to you."

"Yes." said Sam "If you want to leave, we all will." Thomas stood and said,

"This is my sister and I won't let anything harm her."

"We don't want to harm her." said Prince Roderic, tears running down his cheeks, "I just want to save my brother's wife and baby."

"Stop it! Stop it! All of you!" shouted Rebecca once more. "I will help. I want to but no tests." The doctor rose from his chair and stood tall and straight in the light from the windows and said,

"Very vell I, Rebecca and Mrs Gordo will go to the sick room. Ve vill return when we have news." With that he turned to walk from the room looking toward Rebecca with his arm outstretched in a friendly manner. Mrs Gordo stood, took Rebecca by the hand and said,

"Come on, my dear." And they followed Doctor Hitzvelger out of the room. Thomas, Sam and Georgie looked at each other then to Prince Rodric, who was drying his eyes and finally at Gordo.

"Sorry." said Gordo. "I should have told you earlier." They all fell silent looking at the door that Rebecca the Dr and Mrs Gordo had walked through.

Chapter Six

Gone Fishing

Sam, Thomas and Georgie wished that they could have gone with Rebecca. They didn't like the idea of letting her go with Dr. Hitzvelger without them. The fact that Mrs Gordo had also gone along made little difference. Sensing this, Prince Rodric said,

"You need not worry about your sister. I give you my word that no harm will come to her."

"What do we do?" asked Georgie.

"How about something to eat?" offered Tig Tig.

"They have just had breakfast." said Gordo. "This one," he said (pointing to Georgie), "reckons she eats horses."

"What?" exclaimed Tig Tig. "Horses are sacred animals here. Anyone harming them, let alone eating one, is sent to prison!" Sam and Thomas giggled at this as they could see that Georgie was very embarrassed.

"Look." Georgie began to reply. "I don't eat horses. In our world, to say 'I could eat a horse' means you're very hungry. It's just an expression. I love horses. I've been riding since I was about four. I'm quite good now actually. So there!"

"Well," said Tig Tig. "I'm glad we sorted that out. Just don't use that (He paused for effect) expression here!" Georgie glared at Gordo in such a way that he said.

"Sorry, I thought you meant it." Then Prince Rodric spoke.

"I'm very glad that you like to ride," he said "because it's my favourite thing. If you would be so kind as to accompany me, I would like to take you riding."

"Oh, yes please." said Georgie excitedly. The idea of going horse riding with a handsome prince was just too good to be true.

"Good God!" said Sam. "It's just like Ken and Barbie!"

"Be quiet!" Georgie said to him then she turned her attention back to the prince. "Shall we go now?" she asked, thinking, *"Yes! Yes! Right now, on our own! Please! Oh please!"* Prince Rodric, Gordo and Tig Tig had no idea who Ken and Barbie were as they didn't exist in their world. So the Prince asked

"Who are Ken and Barbie?" while he looked around the room in a confused manner. Sam and Thomas were having a good laugh at Georgie's expense again and she didn't like it one bit.

"Will you two be quiet!" she demanded which just made them worse "Never mind about Ken and Barbie. It's just another expression from our world." she said to Prince Rodric. "Let's go, shall we?" And she stood.

"Very well." said Prince Rodric "To the stables. Gordo, look after the boys, will you? I suggest that you take them fishing. One of the boats is leaving shortly to fish in the bay. Tig Tig will stay here and he will contact us if he needs to." So Prince Rodric and Georgie went riding. Gordo rose from his seat and said grumpily.

"Come on then" and walked to the door. Thomas and Sam followed.

"Be sure to let us know if Rebecca needs us." Thomas said to Tig Tig.

"Don't worry; if there is any news, I will let you know." he replied. After leaving the room, Dr. Hitzvelger, Mrs Gordo and, of course, Rebecca headed upstairs, two flights and then along a landing. The door at the end was guarded by two Elfins. They gave Rebecca some very strange looks and did not want either her or Mrs Gordo to pass.

"Sorry Doctor but I have my orders." said the one on the left. "No one passes except you, Prince Rodric and the nurses." Dr. Hitzveleger raised an arm and clicked his fingers, saying,

"Sleptum, Agrantum." At the same time, both guards fell to the ground in an instant; both fast asleep; one snoring quite loudly. The doctor turned to Rebecca and said, "No time to vaste. They vill come to no harm, just a very useful, sleep inducing spell." He opened the door and walked in followed by Mrs Gordo, then Rebecca. Once inside Dr. Hitzvelger dismissed the two nurses. One had been rocking the baby in her cradle. The other had been dabbing the mother's forehead with a cold flannel. The nurses closed the door behind them. Mrs Gordo stood to one side and continued to rock the baby. Dr. Hitzvelger beckoned to Rebecca to come closer to him, next to the bed. Rebecca crossed the room and looked at the Elfin lady in the bed. She was beautiful, even though Rebecca could see that she was very ill.

"What's her name?" asked Rebecca.

"This is the Lady Gwen." answered the doctor "and this is her daughter." he said, pointing to the cradle. "She does not have a name yet. Her father (Lady Gwen's husband) said that if I could save them I could name the

Kevin Gritten

child. So if you can save them I have decided that I vill call the child the princess Rebecca, in your honour." Rebecca smiled and looked into the cradle. She saw a tiny Elfin baby, no bigger than some of her dolls at home. She also looked very ill. "What will you do?" asked the doctor.

"I'm not sure." replied Rebecca. She walked to the bed and took Lady Gwen's hand in hers. She immediately felt warmth between them as with Sam and energy pass between herself and the person she was touching. Rebecca closed her eyes and thought of Narda. Almost at once she could hear Narda's voice in her head.

"Don't be afraid." she said. "Let me help you." Narda's voice was soothing and calming. Rebecca tried to feel her way into Lady Gwen as she had done with Sam. That time she had been able to almost feel herself healing him but this time nothing much was happening. Then Narda's voice came back into her head and she had a startling revelation for Rebecca. "It's not the mother! It's the baby!" Over and over she said it, inside Rebecca's head. "It's not the mother! It's the baby!" Rebecca dropped Lady Gwen's hand and swung around to face the cradle. The action was so quick that she made both Mrs Gordo and Dr. Hitzvelger jump.

"What is it, child?" asked Mrs Gordo.

"Speak Rebecca. vot's wrong?" implored Dr. Hitzvelger.

"It's not the mother making the baby ill!" exclaimed Rebecca. "It's the other way around! It's the baby! She's the one I have to heal!"

Georgie and Prince Rodric talked as they walked to the stables, which were at the end of the village. She found out that Prince Rodric had been shipwrecked and nearly drowned as a boy. The mermaid, Narda had saved him and this was how he knew their story to be true. Georgie told him about home and how they had all ended up in Prince Rodric's village. Before long they were chatting away as though they had been friends forever. They arrived at the stables and stopped to look over a fence, into a wide paddock, where about a dozen horses were grazing. Georgie spotted a beautiful brown and white Pinto on the far side of the paddock.

"Can I ride that one please?" she asked.

"He's quite spirited, that one." answered Prince Rodric.

"I don't care. I want to ride that one." said Georgie.

"As you wish." replied Prince Rodric and he called the groom over. "Make ready my black stallion and the pinto on the other side of the field!" he ordered.

"At once, my lord." came the reply. After a short time both horses were led out, magnificently presented with beautifully handcrafted saddles and tack. Georgie mounted the pinto and the groom handed her a riding whip.

"What's his name?" she asked the groom.

"He's called Lundo, from the old Elfin tongue, which means 'like the wind because he's so fast." the groom answered. "Treat him firmly but give him his head when he wants to run and you will be O.K." Prince Rodric was already astride his black stallion, Hawk. He trotted over to Georgie.

"Shall we go?" he asked and Georgie nodded. Before long they had left the village and were cantering across the fields, heading west towards the mountains.

"Where are we going?" shouted Georgie.

"Sorry, I didn't tell you, did I?" answered Prince Rodric. "If we are to return you all to the world above you must go either over or under the mountains. The best route is over but at this time of the year the snow is falling up there. We have to see if the mountain passes are still open. If not you will have to go under but that means passing through dwarf territory and that's quite a different proposition."

"Gordo told us all about the dwarfs." said Georgie. "They take your people to work in their mines."

"That's right." replied Prince Rodric. "Those who go are seldom seen again."

Sam, Thomas and Gordo were walking towards a small harbour, some distance from the main village and Sam was not in a good mood.

"Fishing! Of all things, fishing!" he said. "This is going to be dead boring." he moaned, as he scuffed his feet along the road.

"Oh stop it Sam." said Thomas. "You don't know that. It might be good fun."

"Fishing? You think fishing will be fun? I'm just going to be bored and fed up."

"If that's how you feel," Thomas said, "and if you're going to be so negative, then go back and wait with Tig Tig. Gordo and I will go fishing on our own. Goodbye." and Thomas walked off in Gordo's direction. Sam scampered to keep up with both of them.

"Well you don't know that it's not going to be boring do you?" Sam said, once he had caught up with them.

"No but at least I'm willing to give it a try." answered Thomas. The two boys had stopped in the road and were facing each other, glaring into each other's eyes; Sam with his arms folded and Thomas with his hands in his pockets. Gordo had also stopped a bit further down the road and was watching the boys with interest.

"You're like a couple of moaning old women." he said. "Do you think I want to go fishing of course not? I'm a forest goblin. We don't like water much. However;"

He continued, "those sailors are great company and they have wonderful food on board ship but the best thing is the really fizzy beer that they brew on board. It's the best in the Elfin lands. Makes me fart, though." he finished. Then he turned and continued to walk down the road. The boys laughed at this last revelation and hurried to catch up with Gordo. Sam not bored at all anymore.

Rebecca looked at Dr. Hitzvelger and said,

"It's the baby. I must hold the baby." The doctor turned to Mrs Gordo and said,

"Give her the child Mrs Gordo." Mrs Gordo pulled back the covers of the cradle and lifted the tiny baby. She then took her to Rebecca and put her into Rebecca's arms. Rebecca could feel at once that this was what she was supposed to be doing. She put her hand on the back of the baby's head and kissed her cheek, saying,

"Don't be frightened. I'm here to help you." Rebecca closed her eyes and thought of Narda. Narda's voice came back to her again.

"That's right, Rebecca." she said. "Hold her and feel her pain disappear as you give her your power and your energy. Rebecca held the baby for a few minutes and she could hear the Lady Gwen stirring in the bed behind her. "That's right." Narda's voice continued in her head. "You're helping them both." It was as if Rebecca could feel the mother and the baby getting stronger by the second. "That's enough now." Narda's voice said. "Put her back in the cradle and try again in an hour." Rebecca gave the baby back to Mrs Gordo, who put her into the cradle.

"Is that it?" asked Dr Hitzvelger.

"Yes, for now." replied Rebecca. "I will try again in an hour."

Georgie and Prince Rodric had made their way up into the mountains. They were now climbing a ridge so that they could overlook the mountain passes below, to see if they were blocked by snowdrifts. They had tethered their horses some way back as they could not make the climb. At the top, Georgie looked around and declared,

"This is one of the most beautiful places I have ever seen."

"Yes, it is rather magnificent isn't it?" Prince Rodric replied. He took a telescope from a bag that he had brought with him and looked down over the edge of the ridge. "We are in luck." he said. "The snow is late this year and the passes are clear."

"Good." said Georgie, "How soon can we leave?"

"That rather depends on Rebecca and how quickly she finishes." answered the Prince.

The boys and Gordo had, by now, reached the harbour and were standing on the quayside, looking at a ship called 'The Tramp'.

"Ahoy there! Anyone on board?" shouted Gordo. A couple of Elfin sailors popped up from below deck and looked at them all with surprise on their faces. Then they disappeared again below deck. Very soon a large, plump Elfin climbed onto the deck and walked towards the plank, which led from the quay onto the ship.

"Ahoy Gordo and how are you? Haven't seen you for ages!" said the plump Elfin. "And my, who are your friends? Human I'll wager."

"That's right." replied Gordo. "This here is Sam and this is Thomas."

"Well, any friend of Gordo is a friend of mine. Come aboard shipmates and tell me what brings you to The Tramp." All three climbed on board and Gordo explained that Prince Rodric had asked Gordo to look after the boys and perhaps take them fishing. He then introduced the elfin to the boys.

"This here is the best captain in the whole Elfin fleet." He proclaimed. "Captain Sorren." The captain laughed and looked to the boys and said.

"Welcome aboard. The crew are just making ready below deck fixing nets and sharpening knifes then we will be ready to sail. Make yourselves comfortable 'til then."

Then he turned and walked off to give orders to some Elfin sailors who had appeared from down below. Captain Sorren, as I have already said, was plump and round. His belly protruded from under his top and hung over his trousers. He had a ring in his belly button, attached to which was what looked to the boys like a shark's tooth. He wore moccasin type shoes, rings in his ears and on his fingers, a scarf around his head and had a goatee beard. Overall he looked like a pirate. After about twenty minutes, with the crew messing about with nets and boards and barrels and lots of other things, the captain gave the order to 'Shove Off'. The Tramp slowly drifted away from the quayside and was soon out of the harbour. Then the sails were raised and the ship sailed out to sea.

Rebecca had been holding the baby and had been trying to make her better every hour. Narda's voice had appeared in her head every time and had helped Rebecca. Rebecca could feel the baby and the mother becoming stronger, every time she held the baby. But, this time, there was no voice and try as she might nothing more seemed to be happening. Then she saw Mrs Gordo's and Dr. Hitzvelger's faces, just looking at the bed in amazement. As Rebecca turned, she could see Lady Gwen, trying to sit up in bed. The baby then started to cry and Mrs Gordo came over to Rebecca and took the child.

"Well done! Oh, well done!" said Mrs Gordo.

"Truly remarkable." added the doctor. Lady Gwen looked at Rebecca and spoke to her.

"It's finished." she said. "You need not try anymore. We are healed, thanks to you."

"How do you know what I did?" asked Rebecca.

"Because I could feel both you and Narda inside me and I could hear your voices in my head."

"Remarkable! Truly remarkable!" said the doctor again.

"You look very tired, my dear." said Mrs Gordo, once the baby was settled with Lady Gwen.

"I am." replied Rebecca. "I think I need a little sleep."

"Mrs Gordo, please take Rebecca to Tig Tig and ask him to find her a room in vhich to sleep." said Dr Hitzvelgar "Stay vith her until she has rested. I vill remain with Lady Gwen and explain exactly vhat has been happening here. Please send the nurses back as vell. Rebecca I vill see you later." Rebecca said goodbye and left with Mrs Gordo. Soon she was snuggled up in a large bed, fast asleep.

Georgie and Prince Rodric were, by now, returning to the village. They were leading their horses on foot and chatting as they walked along. Prince Rodric stopped to pick some wild flowers for Georgie, which she tucked into her saddle. They were surrounded by woodland, which was quite thick in places. As they continued to walk between the trees, the horses started to pull on their reins and seemed to be disturbed by something. Prince Rodric looked concerned.

"What's the matter Rodric?" asked Georgie. Prince Rodric bent to pick some more flowers and then handed them to Georgie as he had done before.

"Stay calm." he whispered. "Re-mount your horse and be prepared to ride hard and don't stop for anything."

"Why? What's wrong?" asked Georgie.

"Dwarfs" Prince Rodric replied. Georgie tried not to show her concern as they both re-mounted as casually as they could. When they were both in the saddle, a loud yell went up from the woods on one side and small men, that Georgie realised were dwarfs, came running towards them. "Go!" Shouted Prince Rodric and they both kicked their horses and sped off as quickly as they could. The dwarfs were quicker though and covered the ground between the wood and the riders very quickly. Most had ropes like lassos, which they spun over their heads and threw at Georgie and Prince Rodric, trying to snare them and bring them down off their horses. Georgie managed to knock one rope away with her free arm and she moved Lundo's head so that another missed him. Then she kicked his side, heading off, sending two dwarfs in front of her flying into the air. At the same time she kicked another dwarf away with her foot. Then she was off, letting Lundo have his head, she sped away. Then she noticed that Prince Rodric wasn't with her so she pulled on the reins, brought Lundo to a halt and turned. Prince Rodric had not been so lucky. One rope had caught the stallion's head and another had caught one of Prince Rodric's arms. The dwarfs were milling around him, punching and pulling him. He was finding it difficult to stay on his horse.

"Go!" He shouted once again. "Save yourself!" Georgie didn't like the look of these dwarfs. They were ugly and mean looking but she couldn't stand the thought of Prince Rodric working in one of their mines. She pulled on Lundo's reins and he reared up on his hind legs. As he came back down and stamped his front hooves into the ground, she let out a murderous scream and pulled the riding crop from her saddle. As we already know a screaming Georgie is something to be reckoned with. All of the dwarfs had stopped to look in her direction, wondering what was about to happen. She screamed again, kicked at Lundo's side and then began to charge back towards the dwarfs who were stunned by the sight for a few seconds. This gave Prince Rodric enough time to free Hawk and himself. By the time Georgie reached Prince Rodric, the dwarfs were trying to re-group themselves for a fight but it was too late. Georgie ploughed into them, scattering them in all directions. Her screams and flailing whip frightened them so much that they ran away and with Prince Rodric free to help, the dwarfs soon gave up.

"Come on!" bellowed Prince Roderic "Back to Tintonia!" So Georgie and the prince rode away as fast as the horses could take them, back to the village.

Soon after leaving the harbour, Captain Sorren gave the order to cast the nets for the first time. The nets were thrown out over the side of the ship by a sort of arm at the front. The arm split into two, throwing the nets to the port and starboard sides. Whilst one was in the sea, gathering fish, the crew would empty the other, beginning to process the fish they had already caught. This involved cutting off their heads and tails and gutting them with a sharp, hooked knife. Both Sam and Thomas were given one and an Elfin sailor showed them what to do. Before long they were gutting fish with the rest of the crew. Gordo stood on the bridge of the ship with the captain keeping an eye on proceedings. The heads, tails and guts were thrown overboard and dark shapes that resembled sharks followed the ship to feed on them. Birds, like gulls also followed to join in this free feast but every now and then one of the dark shapes would jump from the water and take a gull under, sending a shower of water over the side of the ship.

"When the seagulls follow the trawler, it's because they think that sardines will be thrown into the sea." said Thomas.

"Who said that?" asked Sam.

"Eric Cantona." answered Thomas.

"Is he a great wizard, where you come from?" asked an Elfin sailor.

"I'm sure he must have been described as a wizard at sometime." Thomas replied. Sam and Thomas gave each other a knowing smile. Despite the fact that it was dirty, smelly work they were enjoying themselves. All of the Elfins were very friendly and for the first time in days they felt relaxed. They worked hard all day until finally, sometime in the afternoon, Captain Sorren announced that all the barrels below were full and that they could stop fishing and tidy up. Once all the nets were hauled in, the gutting tables cleaned and all stored away, Captain Sorren declared.

"It's time to eat and drink." This was what Gordo had been waiting for and he helped the captain set the table on deck and fill it with fine things to eat and drink. The boys hadn't realised how hungry they were and they tucked in eagerly when told to sit down and start. There was bread and meat, cheese and cake and of course fish but the thing that everyone was looking forward to was the fizzy beer that Gordo had told them about. Both Gordo and the captain were below, getting some barrels of beer for the meal, when someone called Sam's name.

"Did you hear that?" Sam asked Thomas.

"Yes." He replied. "It came from that direction." They heard it again and again so the two boys and the Elfin sailors got up to look. When they peered over the rail of the ship they had quite a surprise.

"Hello, Narda" Said Sam. "How are you?"

"Oh, I'm fine." answered Narda. Then about fourteen other mermaids and mermen popped their heads out of the water. They were all shouting hello to Sam and Thomas. The Elfin sailors were astonished. They had never seen such a thing and, being superstitious, thought this must be some kind of an omen. A good one they supposed. Narda swam close to the ship.

"Rebecca is well." She said. "She has healed the baby and the mother but she is very tired and drained."

"How do you know?" asked Thomas.

"Never mind." said Narda. "Just listen. Sam, take this stone and give it to Rebecca. It will recharge her powers. You may still need them to help you to return home. Keep the stone with you. It has powers of It's own and it will glow for you if danger is near." She handed Sam a black stone which filled his hand and he put it in his pocket.

"Thanks, Narda." he said and with that all the merpeople disappeared below the surface. The Elfin sailors couldn't contain themselves. They all wanted to see the stone and to hear about when the boys had met Narda previously. By now Gordo and the captain had returned and the fizzy beer was flowing into the mugs. The boys liked it very much and Gordo was drinking as much as he could. The captain told the boys how Prince Rodric had also been saved by Narda and that mermaids were the most magnificent things in the land.

"Have you ever seen other humans?" asked Thomas.

"Oh yes." answered the Captain. "Not many though. It's rare in this part of the world. Dr. Hitzvelger's one. If humans stay they don't grow as big down here, but they do grow very wise. That's why they make the best wizards." Then Gordo got up and walked to the ship's stern. He stood there for a while then did the most enormous bottom burp which stopped all conversation at the table. Everyone turned to look at Gordo who said. "Sorry. Beg your pardon" Then did an even louder one which sent the whole table into uncontrollable laughter. Sam and Thomas were almost on the floor. Gordo walked back and sat down.

"It wasn't that funny." he said.

"Oh yes it was." laughed Thomas. Before long everyone was at it. The laughter and revelry continued all the way back to the harbour. Gordo voted Sam Champion Burper and Thomas received rapturous applause for being able to burp and say Manchester United at the same time. Gordo, Sam and Thomas said goodbye on the harbour wall and headed back to the village. Gordo lead the way with Sam and Thomas behind him, singing silly songs like,

'Mary, Mary quite contrary, she's got a big fat bum'.

"Sounds like you're drunk to me" said Gordo.

Chapter Seven

The Naming Ceremony

When Gordo Sam and Thomas arrived back at the village they found Tintonia buzzing with activity. The Elfins were obviously getting ready for some kind of celebration.

"What's going on?" Thomas asked Gordo.

"I've no idea" he answered.

"Look there's Mrs Gordo" said Sam excitedly, pointing to the far side of the village square. "Let's go and ask her." So they all ran across to where Mrs Gordo was making up tables.

"Oh you're back at last" she said as she greeted them. " Just in time. We're having a naming ceremony."

"Naming who?" asked Gordo.

"The baby of course, both she and mother are both doing well, thanks to Rebecca."

"Where is Rebecca now?" asked Thomas.

"Everyone is in the hall. If you and Sam go now you can have a good chat before the ceremony." So Sam and Thomas trotted off toward the hall. Mrs Gordo grabbed hold of Mr Gordo and said accusingly.

"You've been drinking that Elfin beer again haven't you?"

"Only a little drop my love." he answered, sounding a little sheepish.

"You could refuse" countered Mrs Gordo.

"It wouldn't be polite my dear."

"Well I just hope you haven't been teaching those boys bad habits."

"Far as I can see they've got enough of there own" mumbled Gordo. Mrs Gordo ignored this remark and said

"Just one evil smell from your bottom and you can spend the night in the woods! Now help me with these tables."

"Yes my love" said Gordo, knowing that he didn't dare argue. Sam and Thomas entered the room in the great hall where they had been before they went fishing. In the room were Prince Rodric, Georgie, Rebecca, Tig

Tig, Dr Hitzvelgar and an older man the boys had never seen before. The girls ran to the boys and they hugged. None of them had realised quite how much they had missed each other. Sam said to Rebecca

"Look at this. Narda gave it to me. She came right up to our ship, with lots of other Merpeople."

"It's a very pretty stone" remarked Rebecca.

"Narda said it would restore your powers and that I should keep hold of it because it will glow if danger is about." So he gave the stone to Rebecca who held it tight in her hand, all the time thinking of Narda. The stone glowed faintly in her hand and she could feel Narda's power soaking into her once again. When finished the stone lost its glow and Rebecca gave it back to Sam who slipped it into his trouser pocket. That done, Georgie explained to the boys how she and Prince Rodric had found the passes open through the mountains.

"So we can get home that way" she said confidently.

"There is a problem, however" remarked Dr Hitzvelgar.

"The Prince and Georgie were attacked by Dwarfs on the vay home. This can only mean one thing. They know about the four of you. They have guessed we will try to get you home and they mean to stop you." Tig Tig spoke next.

"Dwarfs do not often venture above Ground, not without good reason anyway. They don't like the light a great deal. They obviously think you worth it!"

"We believe, that once on the other side of the mountains, the Dwarfs will try to capture you!" Prince Rodric added.

"So what do we do?" asked Thomas, a worried tone in his voice.

"We have two options as we see it" said Prince Rodric. "We either send an army with you to meet the Dwarfs head on or we send a small group that just might sneak through. This is what we have been discussing."

All fell silent for a while then Sam asked

"Who's he?" pointing to the older man sitting at the table.

"This is professor Mckintey." said Tig Tig "He also came here as a child with the good Dr." Then the professor spoke for the first time.

"We were five in all, Dr Hitzvelgar and myself decided to stay behind. The two girls in our party Helga and Dorothy tried to return by much the same route you will have to take." He took a deep breath then went on. "Dorothy may have been successful but Helga was taken prisoner by the Dwarfs. As far as anyone knows she died in one of their mines."

"What about the fifth person?" asked Thomas.

"He was called Joseph and he tried to go back the way we came."

"Past the giants?" gasped Sam.

"Yes he was seen to be captured by one as soon as he entered the bone fields. We never saw Dorothy again and can only assume she made it home safely."

"This is all very interesting" interrupted Georgie. "But it doesn't get us home does it?"

"I agree" said Prince Rodric. "It's not practical to take an army over the mountains. Also it would take weeks to organise and by then the passes will be closed."

"So we go as a small group then?" asked Thomas.

"Yes we think that's best" agreed Prince Rodric. "Myself, Gordo, Tig Tig and all four of you."

"What about the Dwarfs?" asked Rebecca.

"That's why the professor is here, to see if he had any suggestions" said Prince Rodric. Everyone looked to the professor to hear what he had to say.

"We need something to scare or confuse the Dwarfs. Remember they're not at their best above ground" he said.

"What about a one eyed giant?" offered Sam.

"Vell that vould certainly be an idea." Said Dr Hitzvelgar. "But quite how ve get one to agree I just don't know. I seem to remember you telling me that you stabbed the closest one to us in the bottom with a sword. I think he vould be more inclined to eat you than help."

"Oh that shouldn't be problem" said Professor Mckintey. "One eyed Giants heal very quickly. I shouldn't think it bothered him for long. Mind you they have got terrible tempers."

"What if we offered him some bones?" asked Thomas. "Bones?" everyone replied in unison.

"Yes bones, Dwarf bones. Tell him where the Dwarfs are going to be and say that if he helps he can have as many Dwarfs for bones as he can carry."

"That's horrible!" protested Rebecca.

"So are the Dwarfs" said Georgie.

"What you have to remember is that the Dwarfs would do things just as horrible to the giant if they caught him" said Tig Tig.

"It is a good idea though." Said the Professor. "The giants don't often get the chance to collect Dwarf bones. The Dwarfs won't wander into Giant country and the Giants don't often come down from their lands"

"Assuming that the giant agrees, to help how vill you get him down?" asked Dr Hitzvelgar.

"By using my airship, it has a large basket underneath, big enough for myself, Rebecca, Georgie and the Giant" Said The Professor.

"Why take us?" shrieked the girls.

"Because you Rebecca, can heal the Giant if he is still in pain and Georgie can look after the airship while we talk to Robert."

"Who is Robert?" asked Georgie.

"That's the Giants name" the Professor replied.

"What do Thomas and I do?" quizzed Sam.

"You come with Gordo, Tig Tig and myself, through the mountain pass." Was the answer from Prince Rodric. "We can meet the Professor and the girls and hopefully this Giant called Robert on the other side of the mountains. Once there and all together we can decide best how to deal with the Dwarfs. Now let's all go and join in with the celebrations." They talked a little longer but in the end everyone agreed to the plan, so they took Prince Rodrics advice and went outside to join the fun.

By now things were well under way. The Elfin village was a hive of activity. The children soon found out that Elfins from other villages had come for the celebration, including Prince Rodric's brother whose baby Rebecca had healed. The celebration was a bit like a fair with various stalls all around the square. There were lots of sweets and other things to eat and lots of games to play. At one end of the square there was a long stage on which stood a row of large chairs. All four children were having a great time. Georgie and Rebecca were fascinated by a street magician who was making small objects disappear, then pulling them from someone's pocket or from behind another person's ear. They watched jugglers and acrobats and were given something like candyfloss which was very pleasant to eat. Sam and Thomas were watching Elfins, trying to ride a small wild pig, to see who could stay on the longest. Both Sam and Thomas had a go but were thrown off quite quickly.

"There's obviously a knack to pig riding!" they joked to each other. Then they had a go at a game called stick the Dwarf. This entailed firing crossbows at a model of a Dwarf, made of wood. If you hit the Dwarf in either the nose or the belly button a bell would ring, If you made the bell ring you won a prize. Both Sam and Thomas made the bell ring but were less than impressed when they found the prize was the choice of either a cucumber, a cabbage or a bag of what looked like purple carrots They both took cabbages and gave them to Mrs Gordo who was very pleased. Then there was a rapping from the stage. This turned out to be Dr Hitzvelgar who was using a long wooden staff with a claw shape at the top, in which was held a glowing glass ball, to get everyone's attention. Banging the end of the staff, on the wooden floor, he bellowed.

"All gather around! The naming ceremony is about to begin!" On stage from left to right were Gordo, Professor

Mckintey, Dr Hitzvelgar and Prince Rodrics brother who's name turned out to be Drummond, his wife the lady Gwen, Prince Rodric, Tig Tig and finally two other Elfins the children had not seen before. Everyone in the crowd was now watching the stage and all around was complete silence. Then Dr Hitzvelgar began to speak, "Most of you know vhat has occurred here over the past few days" he started. "Lady Gwen and her child came to us for help but ve could do little. Then the Goblin called Gordo brought the human children to our village and the one called Rebecca healed them both. Ve vill be forever in her debt. So in her honour we have held this naming ceremony, so that all may show their gratitude. Vill you please come to the stage Rebecca?" Rebecca slowly walked up onto the stage looking very shy. While Sam, Thomas and Georgie along with everyone else cheered very loudly. Once Rebecca was on the stage with the Dr he rapped the staff on the floor once more and shouted "Silence!" The baby was in her cradle in front of her mother and father and after he had handed his staff to Professor Mckinty Dr Hitzvelger asked Lady Gwen to pick up the baby for all to see. Then he took the baby from Lady Gwen who sat down again. The Dr held the baby on one arm and took Rebecca by the hand and they walked to the front of the stage. He then held the baby in both hands and holding her high above his head he said.

"By the power vested in me by the Elfin Lords, I hereby name this child The Princes Rebecca." Everyone cheered and clapped and Rebecca felt a little embarrassed by all the attention.

Lady Gwen took the baby back to her chair and began to feed her from a bottle. Prince Drummond then came to the front of the stage and made a short speech in which he thanked the children once again before declaring

"Let the celebrations continue!" Once again there were loud cheers and clapping, then everyone started to wander off to the side shows and stalls to continue the fun. Rebecca and Georgie had great fun helping to look after some of the Elfin children in a kind of crèche. They played dolls with the children and pushed them around in wooden carts and pushed them on makeshift swings. Sam and Thomas found some Elfins playing a ball game they called nets. It was a bit like basketball and was played with two balls four nets and two teams of ten players. After two fiercely contested games they introduced the Elfins to the joys of football. After a quick explanation of the rules, excluding the offside rule, Gordo was elected referee and they played a hard fought game with Sam and Thomas as captains of each side. The game ended up fourteen all and went to penalties. Sam and Thomas started to argue over whether the ball was on the spot or if Tig Tig had put off the penalty taker by dropping his trousers, when Gordo intervened and declared the game a draw. By then it was very late and everyone was drifting off so Mrs Gordo and Tig Tig took the children to their rooms, in the main village building to go to bed. Before long the children were asleep and once again dreaming of home.

Chapter Eight

The Start For Home

The next morning was a glorious one, bright sunshine and a cloudless sky. Professor Mckinty had brought his airship down to the village and it was tethered in a field just outside the large boundary fence. It was still quite early so the only people present were the ones going on the journey. Gordo was in the driving seat of a small wagon which was being pulled by two small horses. This was going to be used by Gordo, Tig Tig, Prince Rodric, Samuel and Thomas to get through the mountain passes.

Georgie and Rebecca were making ready to go with Professor Mckinty up to the Giant Roberts bone field. Sam and Thomas were admiring the large, multicoloured airship and Sam was moaning on about how the girls would have much more fun flying in the airship than he and Thomas would have in the wagon.

"Oh, stop it Sam" said Thomas "It's going to be fun whatever we do. You didn't want to go fishing did you but you enjoyed that didn't you?"

"But flying, that's really cool" replied Sam.

"Yes I agree" answered Thomas. "but they're going up to see the one eyed Giant and that's not so cool is it?" Sam thought about this then replied,

"You're right, I didn't think about that. Perhaps the wagon won't be so bad after all." Just then Professor Mckinty came walking over from his airship.

"Morning boys" he said in a very jolly manner.

"Morning" they chorused.

"Now Sam, you have your stone from Narda and Rebecca has her gift of healing also from Narda. I think it's time to give Thomas and Georgie something." He was carrying a small leather bag and he gave it to Thomas to hold after he had taken a white circular piece of wood from it. "This is for you Thomas, It's a sort of compass. Hold it in your hands like so and just ask it a question." He held it flat and asked "Which way to the Giant's bone field?" The white face of the wood turned smokey and then a compass face appeared, with the arrow pointing west, then it vanished and the wood returned to white. "See, it's very easy and it will guide you in the right direction when you are past the Dwarfs."

"What about Georgie?" asked Sam.

"Oh Prince Rodric has something for her" said the Professor. Georgie and Rebecca were by the wagon with Tig Tig and the Prince. The girls were saying their goodbyes before heading off in the airship with the Professor.

"Don't worry" said Prince Rodric. "We will see you again on the other side of the mountains."

"I hope so." replied Rebecca, "I don't much like the idea of going to see the Giant again!"

"You will be o.k. with the Professor" said the prince calmly. "Now Georgie, I have something for you." He took a smallish length of curved wood from one of his jacket pockets. "This is what you would call a boomerang in your world I believe but what we call a wizzer. Just look at what you want to hit, focus on it in your mind and throw. It never misses and it always comes back. It might prove useful where you are going."

Everyone shook hands hugged and finished their goodbyes, then Sam and Thomas got into the back of the wagon with Tig Tig. Prince Rodric got up onto the front of the wagon with Gordo and they set off for the mountains. Georgie and Rebecca got into the airship basket with Professor Mckinty and he cast off the ropes holding the airship. They gradually rose up into the air and the Professor steered a course for the bone field with the girls looking very anxious beside him. The going for everyone in the wagon was very rough and bumpy but before long they were into the mountains and well on their way. The journey by airship however was much more enjoyable for everyone concerned. Flying above the clouds, they made good progress and before long they could see the Giant's bone field below them.

"Time to throw out the anchor and winch ourselves down" said Professor Mckinty. With that he opened a hatch in the bottom of one end of the basket. Above it hung a shiny anchor like on a ship. He pulled a lever and the anchor sailed down, through the opening and struck the ground with a loud, satisfying thud scattering two piles of bones.

"Oh great." said Georgie "That Giant's really going to be pleased with us for messing up his bone collection again."

"Don't worry about Robert" said Professor Mckinty as he winched in the anchor chain, which drew the airship closer to the ground. "He'll be O.K. when he knows it's me."

"Do you know this Giant well Professor?" asked Rebecca.

"Oh yes, I trade vegetables, wood and Elfin beer with him" answered the Professor.

"What for?" asked Rebecca.

"Mostly for things that fall into this world from the world above" said the Professor. "I used to trade with another called Dennis but he seems to have moved on."

"He didn't move on." said Georgie "We found a pile of bones with a label on them saying 'my brother Dennis' when we were here before."

"Oh dear, oh dear, oh dear" said Professor Mckinty "That's the problem with these one eyed Giants. They have such tempers and they just don't get on together. That's why there's not many of them left." These remarks didn't fill the girls with confidence but they didn't say anything to the professor. Once the airship was on the ground and secure all three clambered out. They stood in the bone field for a while. Then the Professor went to get something from the airship while Goergie and Rebecca looked at some of the labels on the bones close by. Georgie read one to Rebecca which said.

"My Auntie Petunia! Gosh they really don't get on do they?"

'This one says 'a human called Joseph' said Rebecca. "We'd better not tell the Professor we've found his friend"

Kevin Gritten

"No, best not" agreed Georgie. "This one says Lord Longford"

"Listen to this one" said Rebecca "The Queen of Hearts."

"I think he must make some of these up" said Georgie. Then the Professor was back and he was carrying a megaphone.

"There this should get his attention" said the Professor in a confident tone. He put the megaphone to his lips and shouted through it. "Robert, come on Robert where are you? It's Professor Mckinty here, can you hear me?" There was no answer but they could hear a thumping sound in the distance which was getting closer. Then they realised the thumping was footsteps, giant footsteps. "Is that you Robert?" asked the Professor through the megaphone.

"Of course it is." came the reply. "You don't have to shout either, I may have only one eye but I can hear perfectly well!" They could see him in the distance now heading their way at great speed. For a big fellow he could move very quickly.

"I'm frightened" said Rebecca with a whimper.

"Don't worry." the Professor said "I've told you, you will be O.K. with me." All three fell silent as the giant approached. They could see the look of surprise and horror appear on Robert's face as he drew closer to them and he realised who was with the Professor. He came very close then roared,

"I want those two and the boys wherever they are! One of them stuck a sword in my bottom you know."
"Yes, yes, yes I do know as it happens but lets just forget that for a moment shall we?" said Professor Mckinty.

"Forget it" roared Robert who sounded like he had a bit of a head cold. "You try and forget something like that! It still hurts now, right down to the bone." Then as if confirming the cold theory, he sneezed "aaachooow" he roared and then said apologetically "sorry" then wiped his nose on his sleeve. He then looked at the Professor, Georgie and Rebecca and realised that he had sneezed all over them. There they stood all covered in snot and bogies. "Oh dear what have I done" he said.

"That's it!" shouted Rebecca. "You must be the most disgusting creature I have ever met. You're smelly, rude, you've got spots and warts and I bet you don't wash your pants!"

"What are pants?" asked Robert looking toward Professor Mckinty.

"Well there," he began to answer but Rebecca was in full flow and was not going to be stopped.

"Never mind that now!" she yelled. "Just turn around and bend over right now."

"My, my," said Professor Mckinty to Georgie "she is a spirited young thing isn't she?"

"I've never seen her so angry" replied Georgie. Robert was just standing looking at the Professor.

"You had better do as you have been told" the Professor said to Robert. So the giant turned around and bent over. Rebecca walked up to him and said.

"The last thing I wanted to do today was put my hand on a giant's bottom." There was a split in his trousers with a blood stain around it. It had been badly sewn and even though she didn't want to, she put her hand on it and thought of Narda. Immediately she could feel herself healing the giant; not just his bottom but his cold, spots, warts and all. When Rebecca had finished she stood back and said. "Yuk, ulcers and bad breath too. You really were in a mess."

"How do you feel now Robert?" asked Professor Mckinty.

"I feel great!" he answered and let out a huge roar.

"Good, now you can do something for us." said Georgie.

"What do you want me to do?" asked Robert, looking at Georgie with a rather worried expression on his face.

"We want you to come with us." she started to explain. "We're all trying to get home but the Dwarfs are trying to stop us. If you could help us get past the Dwarfs you can have as many as you can carry back." The Giant's eyes lit up and he smiled.

"Dwarfs?" he growled.

"Yes, Dwarfs" said the Professor.

"Dwarfs from under nightmare mountain." again Robert's eyes lit up. "Oh, nightmare mountain, those are really tasty" said Robert licking his lips. "Just wait here a minute while I nip back for some sacks!" and off he went.

"Well I think that went rather well don't you?" said Professor Mckinty.

"For you maybe!" exclaimed Rebecca "but I can still taste him yuk!" They waited for a short while then Robert returned with two large sacks, wearing a balaclava.

"What's that for?" asked Goergie, trying not to laugh.

"My mum always told me to wrap up warm if I left this place. She knitted me this balaclava." The balaclava was black with one hole for Roberts mouth and one for his large single eye. It made him look very strange.

"Well, let's get on shall we?" said Professor Mckinty and before long they were all aboard the airship, heading toward nightmare mountain.

Chapter Nine

The Dwarfs And The Bizerker

Sam, Thomas, Prince Rodric, Tig Tig and Gordo's journey through the mountains was mostly uneventful but the going was very slow in the wagon. Gordo had brought along two barrels of Elfin beer. He had traded them for some tree wax that Captain Sorren used for waterproofing his ship The Tramp. Consequently part of the way through the journey, the beer began to flow and everyone was feeling very merry. You can imagine the sorts of songs they were all singing. Not to mention the smells and noises that were mixing with their merry tunes as the wagon travelled through the mountain passes. It took them two whole days to get through the mountains and some of it was very frightening. When they were going up, the road became very narrow and if they looked to the side, the road just dropped away. All they could see was a vast deep cavern with jagged rocks at the bottom and Gordo had to be very steady with the horses and wagon at these points. They had consumed all of the Elfin beer by this stage which was probably a blessing. When they were past the worse and on their way down the other side of the mountain Sam asked Gordo.

"Will we get there first?"

"Goodness no, the others would have been there a while now."

"Do you think they will be O.K.?" Thomas asked Prince Rodric.

"Yes I think so. Remember they have got the giant Anyway the Dwarfs want you all so I do not think they would try anything until you are all together." A few hours later they were out of the mountains and on much more level ground. The sun shone in the sky and in the distance they could see Professor Mckinty's airship moored by a large lake.

Georgie, Rebecca, Professor Mckinty and Robert had made a camp beside the road which went around the edge of the lake. On the other side of the camp was a ridge so the camp was well hidden. As the wagon drew closer they could see Georgie, Rebecca and the professor waving furiously. Robert, the giant was asleep on a huge rock using a bush he had uprooted for a pillow. Once the wagon was in camp everyone jumped down and the two weary bands of travellers exchanged pleasantries and laughed and joked for a while. Gordo looked at the professor and said

"Looks like you were successful." nodding his head toward Robert.

"Oh yes" replied the professor who then proceeded to tell them all the whole story with the help of Georgie and Rebecca. When he had finished Prince Rodric asked,

"Have you seen any Dwarfs?"

"Not yet." answered Georgie.

"I'm going to take a look at the view from the top of that ridge," announced Thomas. Then, when everyone looked at him, he added, "To use the compass and see which way is home. You coming Sam?"

"You betcha!" replied Sam enthusiastically.

"I think I will come too." said Tig Tig, So all three started to climb the ridge. Halfway up the ridge, Sam shouted in a rather concerned tone,

"Look you two my stone!" They turned to see Sam holding his stone in his hands and it was glowing. "The further we go up the ridge, the brighter it glows. It's getting warmer too."

"I don't like the sound or the look of that." said Tig Tig.

"Well let's not stop now let's get to the top and see what's on the other side of this ridge." said Thomas and he resumed his climb. When they did reach the top, the sight before them was awesome and quite frightening. Sam's stone was, by now, glowing bright blue and all three could see why. On the other side, the ridge dropped down again, then rose up and formed a sort of plateau. On the other side of the plateau were trees and beyond that more mountains. Standing on the plateau was the Dwarf army, hundreds of them all lined up and ready to fight. To the right, at the rear of the Dwarf army, on a large mound, the three travellers could make out four figures mounted on donkeys.

"That's Nightmare Mountain in the distance." said Tig Tig, pointing to beyond the trees.

"Do you think they have seen us?" asked Thomas.

"I doubt it. They don't see very well above ground. I expect they can smell us though. They have a very keen sense of smell, do Dwarfs."

"So they're just waiting for us to make the first move then?" asked Sam.

"That would be my guess" replied Tig Tig.

"Come on Thomas. Use the compass and see which way we have to go. Maybe we can make a run for it" urged Sam. So Thomas took the compass from it's bag, held it flat in his hand and asked,

"Which way is home?" Immediately the compass face appeared and pointed to the east. "It wants us to follow the road around the plateau." said Thomas. "Can we make it without being seen?" Thomas asked the compass. Sam thought he was mad asking the compass that question but the compass face disappeared and the word *No* in red capital letters appeared instead.

"I guess that's a no then?" Joked Sam and all three laughed. By now Prince Rodric and the others had joined the boys and Tig Tig at the ridge's edge. Robert was still asleep on his rock, snoring lightly.

"Oh dear, oh dear" mumbled Gordo "There are far too many of them to fight." Prince Rodric was looking through his telescope and said,

"It's worse than that. They have a bizerker with them!" Gordo, Tig Tig and the professor looked terrified when they heard this news.

"What's a bizerker?" asked Georgie.

"It's a cross between a goblin and a dwarf" answered Prince Rodric. "He's the hairy one at the back on the donkey." Georgie and all the others had a quick look through the telescope, to see. They saw an ape like creature sitting on a donkey with a huge axe in it's hand. He had no clothes but was covered in thick black hair. His head was huge and Sharp teeth stuck out of his mouth.

"They have no fear and they fight for whoever pays the most" said Gordo.

"I'm not sure even Robert could handle a bizerker?" said Professor Mckinty. Prince Rodric was again looking through his telescope.

"This one is one of the Worst. They call him The Butcher" he said to the others. "The dwarf (on the donkey to the front of the group) is the Dwarf King Maximums Oberon Stoat. Although most people just call him Max. He's one of the most wicked dwarf kings."

"You mean there's more than one?" shrieked Rebecca.

"Oh yes, lot's." said Prince Rodric.

"Looks like we're up against it" said Gordo and added, "I hope Robert's in the mood for a fight?" While this conversation was in progress, Sam had been juggling his stone in one hand. He was feeling rather fidgety, shuffling around on his bottom. He had this unexpected urge to throw his stone at the dwarfs.

"Do you need to go to the toilet?" Georgie asked him.

"No I went before we came up here, behind that bush." he said, pointing. "No, what I want to do is this."

He stood up in full view of the Dwarf Army. At once the Dwarfs began to bang their weapons against their shields and shouted and bawled. The Bizerker, called The Butcher, had to be stopped from riding off after Sam.

"That's it Sam. You take them on all by yourself!" said Gordo rather sarcastically. Sam just ignored him, raised his arm and threw the stone straight at the Dwarf Army. As he did he let out a huge scream and yelled,

"Take that, you ugly lot!" Then three things happened. Robert woke up, the dwarfs went quiet and the stone hurtled toward them at a incredible speed. It went further and faster than Sam could ever have imagined it would. All the others on the ridge now stood up and watched in amazement. The stone was almost upon the dwarfs and the dwarfs directly in it's path were getting ready to jump out of the way when it veered off and shot straight up into the air. It stopped above them hovering in a menacing sort of way. After a few moments the dwarfs started to laugh and jeer at Sam and the others on the ridge. Then the king gave the order for all his army to move forward and the dwarfs set off at a walk.

"Now look what you have done!" said Thomas to Sam.

"It's not my fault. I just wanted to knock them all over." Sam replied. With that, the stone shot back down to earth at top speed. It hit one dwarf on the head then another in the middle of his back. Then it continued to shoot around knocking dwarfs flying in all directions.

"I knew it would do that." laughed Sam.

"Of course you did." said Thomas then added, "I don't think." They both laughed heartily as they watched the stone continue it's rampage. Gordo, Tig Tig, Prince Rodric and Professor McKinty were surveying the scene in complete disbelief. Rebecca turned to Georgie and said

"Why not try your wizzer, Georgie?"

"I was just thinking the same Thing." So she took the gift from her pocket and looked toward the Dwarf Army. Sam's stone appeared to be doing a fine job on its own. So Georgie turned her attention to the mound. Where the King Dwarf, his guard and The Bizerker called the Butcher were still sitting on their donkeys. She looked at the hairy Bizerker and took good aim. Then she threw her wizzer with all her might, keeping her eyes fixed upon the Bizerker. The wizzer shot off even faster than Sam's stone.

"Cor did you see that Thomas?" shouted Sam. The wizzer sped across the top of the Dwarf Army, toward the mound and hit The Bizerker who Prince Rodric called the Butcher, right between the eyes. He fell off the back of his donkey and lay motionless on the ground, completely unconscious. The wizzer bounced off the Butcher and hit the Dwarf King, Maximums Oberon Stoat, on the back of the head. He lurched forward and fell head first over his donkey's head. He was also left unconscious. The remainder of the dwarfs on the mound rode away as quickly as they could with what was left of the Dwarf Army following, in complete disarray. By now, Robert had reached the top of the ridge, just in time to see Georgie's wizzer doing it's job. When the dwarfs saw the giant Robert they ran even faster to get away from the battlefield.

"You started without me" he complained.

"Well go after them," said Tig Tig, all matter of fact. "If you hurry you can catch a Bizerker. He's over there on that mound, unconscious."

"Really?" said Robert eagerly. "O.K. I'm off. Have a safe journey home, you kids" and with that he tore off after the dwarfs, his sacks flapping behind him.

"Right, let's get you four on your way. We must not waste anymore time!" Prince Rodric shouted above the noise from the battlefield.

"The compass said to go in that direction." Thomas replied.

"Very well, all of you into the wagon, Tig Tig, Gordo, Professor McKinty and myself will use the airship to get back to Tintonia."

"What about Robert?" asked Rebecca.

"Oh he will be O.K. He can take the long way home, through the hills" answered the Professor.

"Who's going to drive the wagon?" asked Thomas.

"I will." said Georgie "I've driven a horse and trap at riding school." Georgie had by now caught the wizzer, which had flown back, after hitting the Dwarf King. Sam had also retrieved his stone by yelling,

"Come back stone!" Much to every-one's surprise it had obeyed his command immediately and flown to his outstretched hand. The four children clamoured into the wagon, with Georgie up front, driving. Thomas sat beside her with the compass while Sam and Rebecca made themselves comfortable in the back. They waved and shouted their goodbyes to their friends, who were climbing into the basket of the airship. Georgie shouted

"Giddy up horsy." and the wagon set off in the direction that Thomas's compass had said they should go. As they made their way along the road, they could see Robert struggling to put dwarfs into his sacks. He was having a terrible problem with one that the children thought might have been The Bizerker. Looking back they could see the airship rising into the air and heading off in the opposite direction. Once again they were on their own and they felt a little nervous. Having spent so much time with the Elfins and having made so many friends, they felt very sad to be leaving. So for a little while they were all very quiet as they made there way toward the edge of a very forbidding looking forest.

Chapter Ten

Topo
The Nicest Mices

They spent the rest of that day travelling along the very bumpy, stoney road. It was hard going and by nightfall they were all very tired. They spent a restless night in the wagon listening to all the noises of the night outside the wagon. Some noises were familiar to them like the hooting of owls. Others like the huge roar that woke them all at one point were not. There was plenty of food, water and blankets to keep them warm so they were quite cosy but this did not stop them from feeling very frightened. Their spirits were restored however by the rising of the morning sun. Their they stood by the wagon, Sam, Georgie and Rebecca watching Thomas with the compass.

"Which way now?" Thomas asked the compass. The compass pointed in the same direction along the road.

"This is getting boring" moaned Sam. "How far do you think we have to go now?" he asked Thomas yawning.

"I don't know, I'll ask?" answered Thomas. "How far to go now?" Thomas asked the compass. *Far Enough!* came the reply written on the face of the compass.

"Well that doesn't help very much does it?" said Georgie.

"Come on, let's get going there's no point in hanging around here." said Rebecca, trying to sound enthusiastic. So they all clambered aboard the wagon once again and set off down the same road. About two or three miles down the road the compass face suddenly came to life again and pointed to the right. They had been following the road with a thicket of trees on their right hand side. Now there appeared to be a break in the trees on that side and the compass indicated with a bright blue arrow that it wanted them to go that way.

"I don't want to go into the forest," complained Rebecca. "The last time it was full of bad fairies."

"Yes and they bite." added Sam.

"Do we have to go that way?" Thomas asked the compass. *Yes* was the reply. "Is there another way?" he asked. *No* was the reply this time.

"Oh well, looks like we don't have a choice." said Georgie and she turned the wagon off the road and onto the path through the trees. The going was even tougher there and eventually the wagon became bogged down in the mud. Try as they may, pushing and pulling they could not shift it. Worse than that though was the fact that it had begun to rain.

"That's it." said Sam "We will have to go on by foot and try to find some shelter."

"Shouldn't we stay in the wagon tonight?" said Thomas.

"We can't. It's beginning to sink" Sam pointed out.

"You boys grab what you can. Rebecca and I will set the horses free. Come on Becks before the wagon disappears."

"Will they be able to find their way home?" Rebecca asked Georgie.

"I don't know but Prince Rodric said to let them go when we couldn't use them anymore." The boys put all they could carry into four bags, saving the largest ones for themselves. Thomas then asked the compass which way to go and they set off again on foot. The horses ran off in the opposite direction and the wagon continued to sink until only the very top was visible. After a short spell of walking they came to an old shack on the edge of a clearing. The shack was built into the side of a rocky outcrop that seemed to go up into the sky without stopping. Further along from the shack was the entrance to a cave. Thomas looked at his compass and asked

"Do we have to go into the cave?" *Yes,* came the reply *but wait until morning*

"I vote we use the shack until then. I bet the compass has been leading us to it all along." said Sam.

"Come on then, I'm cold and wet." said Rebecca shivering. Georgie was first through the door of the shack and said to the others.

"It's quite cozy in here. let's see if we can start a fire." So Georgie and Rebecca set about starting a fire in the grate at one end of the shack. Once started they used a pan to cook sausages that they had brought from the wagon. The boys made up beds at the other end of the shack. The shack didn't look like it had been used for a very long time but it felt safe and was soon warm and full of the smells of cooking that made the children's mouths water. Once they had warmed up, eaten and dried out they began to chat about their adventure so far.

"How long do you think we have been away?" Georgie asked Thomas.

"I'm not sure. About a week I would guess," he answered.

"I bet Mum and Kevin are missing us." said Rebecca.

"We are going to be in so much trouble." said Sam, grinning from ear to ear.

"Well there's no need to sound so happy about it." sparked Thomas. All the others just looked at him. "Look they're probably worried sick, we've never been away this long. All we can do is get back as quickly as we can." was the best Thomas could manage.

"We're still going to be in a lot of trouble." said Sam again and everyone grinned with him this time.

"What day was it when we were by the lake and fell into the hole?" Rebecca asked everyone.

"Saturday." answered Thomas.

"That means we've missed a week of school!" exclaimed Rebecca. They all laughed and cheered at this.

"I wonder how they explained that to the teachers." said Georgie.

"I bet the police and every-one's been looking for us. I bet we've even been on the news!" added Sam.

"I do hope we get home soon." said Rebecca sounding very tired and sad.

"Don't worry sis, I'm sure we will be." said Thomas trying to sound confident. After a bit more chat they settled down for another night's rest, which was only broken by Sam's loud snores. Rebecca and Georgie had to cover their heads with blankets. Thomas, owing to him having to share a room with Sam at home was used to it. Anyway, Thomas could sleep through almost anything. In the morning they all ate goats cheese and bread before packing up their blankets and what was left of their supplies. Then they ventured outside into what was a bright, sunshiny day.

"Into the cave then." said Sam and he walked into the darkness before them. Almost at once light came from the walls around him.

"It's just like the tunnels we went through before." remarked Rebecca as she joined Sam.

"Look at the wall." gasped Georgie as she walked into the tunnel. They all turned to see what Georgie was pointing at. On the wall of the tunnel was writing in big letters that proclaimed. *DOROTHY WAS HERE.*

"Professor Mckinty was right" said Thomas "She did make it."

"Well she got this far anyway" agreed Sam.

"Come on, let's get going." said Rebecca and she walked off in quite a confident manner. The tunnel was very like the ones they had been in before so no one was worried. They just kept walking at a brisk pace.

"It's a good thing the professor gave you that compass." Sam said to Thomas. "We would never have found this tunnel otherwise."

"It would have been a lot harder for sure" agreed Thomas.

"I wonder how Dorothy found it?" said Georgie.

"Good point! Perhaps she had a compass too" wondered Sam.

"I think I can see the end up ahead!" shouted Rebecca. They were all very tired and were still carrying the supplies they had brought from the wagon but they speeded up to get to the end. They came out into a huge chamber. They could not see the top but it was bright and very cool. There were five other tunnels leading from the chamber and all looked the same.

"Shall I do eaney meany miney mo again?" joked Sam.

"I think Thomas should ask the compass this time." said Rebecca meaningfully. So, once again Thomas held the compass in his hand and asked a question of it.

"Which way home?" The compass face clouded then words began to appear. *Five Tunnels From Left To Right, Take Away Three And Hold On Tight.*

"What's that supposed to mean? said Sam.

"Oh that's easy." said Georgie. "Count the tunnels from left to right." she counted. "One, two, three, four, five. Then take away three. One two three and you're left with two, so it must be tunnel number two."

"Sounds good to me." said Thomas.

"Hold on." said Sam. "It says from left to right, if you take away three from the left, you get to tunnel number four. I think it's that one."

"He has a point." Thomas said to Georgie.

'"I think it's tunnel number three." said Rebecca. All the others turned to look at her and Thomas asked,

"Why?"

"Well if you count three from the right, you end out on tunnel three. If you count three from the left, you get to tunnel three so I think it's that one."

"I'm confused" said Thomas. So he asked the compass

"Which way should we go, tunnel two, three or four?" The compass face clouded then the image of a tiny man rose from the wood, dressed in top hat and tails, carrying a cane. He did a little tap dance around the surface of the compass that held the children mesmerized. Then he stopped, looked at Thomas and began to speak.

"Four, three or two, the choice is up to you. Only the one who holds the compass can pick. So follow my cane but remember be quick." With that he threw his cane toward the tunnels and disappeared back into the compass face. His cane sped through the air and flew into tunnel number two.

"See, I told you so." boasted Georgie triumphantly. Then all the tunnel entrances began to close.

"Come on! Hurry, he said we had to be quick!" shouted Thomas. They ran as if their lives depended on it, (which they probably did). Thomas and Georgie made it into the tunnel, together with Sam just behind but Rebecca tripped on a stone and fell. She screamed and shouted

"Don't leave me!" Sam was the closest and turned to see her lying in the dirt. He knew he would have to be quick but he could not leave Rebecca. So he ran back, pulled her up by one arm and hoisted her over his shoulder in a fireman's lift. Then, with Rebecca still screaming at the top of her voice, he ran for the closing entrance. Georgie and Thomas were on the other side of the door, trying to push it back with all there strength, urging Sam to be quick. He ran as fast as he could with Rebecca still struggling on his shoulder. The door was almost closed when Sam lurched forward and rolled, with Rebecca, through what was left of the gap in the door. Thomas and Georgie jumped back and the door closed with a loud bang behind them. All went pitch black for a second then the light began to seep from the walls again. Once their eyes had adjusted they could again see the way ahead. They could also see that Sam had landed in the only muddy patch to be seen, so once again he was the messiest of them all. They all had a little laugh about this. Rebecca thanked Sam for helping her then they continued their journey into the tunnel. The tunnel wasn't lengthy and before long they were walking out into a bright, cartoon landscape. It was most bizarre. There they were real people on a cartoon background. There were fields and streams, woods and in the distance a village. Birds flew, bees buzzed and all in all it was quite a pleasant scene. In front of them was a grey road, leading down to a bridge, over a stream. On the bridge stood two creatures. Quite what they were the children couldn't see from where they stood so they started to walk toward them. They could see that one was jumping up and down and that the other was leaning against the rail of the bridge. As they drew nearer to the bridge they began to make out who or rather what these new creatures were. The one jumping up and down was a large mouse carrying a red handbag and dressed in a matching bright red jacket with elaborate black braiding. The other was a large teddy bear. He was reading a paper and smoking a pipe. He was wearing shorts, a waist coat and big boots.

"Oh look, see! "They heard the mouse say in a very squeaky voice "It's humans children's. oh goodies!" She squeaked continuing to jump up and down at a terrific rate.

"Be still" said the teddy. "Don't get so excited." Then he returned to his paper and pipe. As they drew closer to the bridge the mouse shouted out to them.

"Comes on children's. Hurries. We've beens waitings for you."

"Don't rush them they have plenty of time." said the bear.

"Time for what?" asked Thomas as they walked onto the bridge and came face to face with the teddy and the mouse.

"All in good time young man, all in good Time." answered the bear. Then he smiled at them and said. "First, introductions. My name is Alexander Donald Sigmund Brown. You can all call me Alex, for short, everybody does." Then he tapped out his pipe and put it in his pocket.

"My names is Topo I'm ones ofs the nicest mice's. We'ves beens waitings for yous."

"She talks a bit like Rebecca." Sam whispered to Thomas. Thomas sniggered a bit, then perfectly on time Rebecca stepped forward and laughed,

"Oh I likes the nicest mice's." then she and Topo began to bounce Together, both clapping their hands.

"How did you know we were coming?" asked Georgie.

"A bell sounds as soon as anyone enters the tunnel to here." answered Alex The Bear.

"We'ves beens waiting ever since!" added Topo bouncing up and down excitedly.

"Why? Are you our guides? What do we have to do now? demanded Thomas.

"All you need to know, at the moment, is that you are nearly home." replied Alex. "However, you do have to complete a task while you are here before you can proceed."

"I don't like the sound of that." whispered Sam to Thomas.

"Come on follow me" said Alex The Bear as he walked over the bridge and onward, down the grey road. Rebecca followed hand in hand with Topo, chatting and bouncing away as only they could. Thomas, Sam and Georgie tagged along behind, feeling rather apprehensive about the whole situation they now found themselves in.

"They seem very friendly but I suggest we keep our wit's about us" said Thomas to Sam.

"I agree" said Sam "I don't like the way that mouse is with Rebecca."

"I know what you mean Sam" said Georgie. "I can't quite put my finger on it but I feel very uneasy about all of this."

"Just keep your eyes peeled for trouble both of you" said Thomas, Sam and Georgie nodded their agreement.

"Come on keep up not far to go" called Alex the Bear

Chapter Eleven

Fire And Water

They walked some way, going away from the village. They could see in the distance that everything was still a cartoon world, even the birds and bees that darted here and there. The road they walked along was a cartoon road and they even saw a cartoon train making it's way toward the village. The only things that seemed real were themselves Alex and Topo (if you can call a giant mouse and a talking teddy bear real). They eventually walked into a gorge and as they walked, the sides grew higher and higher. It was a dead end and the children were in for a surprise. In front of them was a hole in the rock face like another tunnel entrance. A raging fire blocked this hole.

To their right was a pond or small lake. On the water floated wooden platforms. They were joined together by planks of wood attached by chains. It was obvious what you had to do. By crossing the planks between the wooden squares you could make your way to the other side. The only problem being that every ten seconds or so the water would rise up violently and wash over the planks with great force. All the children could see that, if caught on the planks, a person could be washed off and would disappear into the water. It was also very apparent that the fire and water were both very real.

"Now I am sure you can all see what you have to do," said Alex. "Cross the water, using the wooden platforms but be careful. Only one plank between each float is the correct route. Use the wrong one and it will try and tip you into the water. When you reach the other side you will find a lever in the rock face. Simply pull the lever down and the waves will stop. You can then use any route you choose to return. The lever will also turn off the fire at the tunnel entrance. That is your way home." Alex stopped to look at the children to see if they had taken in everything that he had told them, then Topo spoke.

"Bees quicks though yous only haves twenty seconds on each planks or it wills throws yous offs!"

"Any questions?" asked Alex

"How many goes do you get?" asked Sam.

"One each" replied Alex.

"What happens if you fall into the water?" asked Thomas.

"You become statues, in our museums" replied Topo eagerly.

"You have two minutes to decide who will go first" said Alex firmly. The children huddled around each other so that Topo and Alex could not hear them talking.

"Who will go first then?" Georgie asked.

"Not me!" pleaded Rebecca.

"It's obvious." said Sam. "Thomas has the compass. He can ask it which plank to take on each float, while the water washes over, then move to the next one. It's our only hope." Sam, Georgie and Rebecca all looked at Thomas.

"O.K. it's me but I'm beginning to wish that I didn't have this thing." He held up the bag containing the compass not looking too happy.

"Have you made a choice?" asked Alex The Bear.

"Yes," replied Georgie "Thomas will go first." Alex beckoned to Thomas saying

"Come on then Thomas. Let's get started." Thomas walked with Alex to the edge of the water then Alex prompted him to move out onto the first floating platform. Thomas watched the water washing over the planks to try and get an idea of the timing of each wave. Alex watched him then shouted,

"The trial starts now." Thomas quickly took the compass from it's bag and held it flat in his hands. Then he asked it,

"Which way?" The compass arrow appeared and pointed to the left-hand plank. As the water subsided, Thomas walked to the next float and repeated the process. Using this method, he was soon making his way across the water.

"What's he gots in his hands, Alex?" asked Topo.

"I'm not sure," he replied "but I do think he must be cheating. I think I will call him back and make him start again."

"Oh no's, don'ts do that, just tips him into the waters." She shrieked excitedly.

"Hold on a minute!" shouted Sam in amazement. "You can't do that. You didn't say he couldn't use his compass to get across. You just said he had to get there."

"That's right!" screamed Georgie and Rebecca in unison. Alex and Topo turned away and seemed to be discussing the situation. It the meantime, Thomas only had a short way to go before he reached the other side of the water. Rebecca was cheering him on

"Go on Thomas! go,! go!" she yelled. Sam turned to Georgie and said,

"Get ready with your wizzer. If it looks like they're going to drop Thomas in the water, you hit the mouse and I will use my stone on the teddy. Got that?"

"O.K." replied Georgie. They both turned to keep an eye on Topo and Alex, to see what they would do next.

"You're right," remarked Alex, as he turned back to face the children. "There's nothing in the rules to say you can't use an aid to help you complete the trial."

"Last times it's was a little girls and she had a silvers birds to help hers." said Topo.

"Was her name Dorothy?" asked Georgie.

"Don't know." replied Alex but then again we didn't ask you your names did we?"

"I bet it was Dorothy" Georgie whispered to Sam.

"Look all of you. He's nearly there." came the triumphant shout from Rebecca, who had been watching her brother intensely. Thomas was only two platforms away from the far side of the water. However, the waves were increasing in frequency and force. He was finding it hard to hold the compass still, long enough to see which plank to cross. With cheers coming from the others on the bank he guessed and rushed across a plank to the last float. He had guessed correctly and just in time, as the platform he had been on tried to tip him into the water as he moved to the next one. The water, was now becoming very choppy and waves splashed over the floats and planks. Thomas could hardly keep his footing and it was impossible for him to read the compass. Time was running out and he had to make a decision as to which plank to take to reach the other side. He took a quick look over his shoulder at the others who had all gone strangely quiet and replaced the compass in its leather bag. He then drew in a deep breath and jumped onto one of the planks using it as a springboard to push off with a giant leap to reach the other bank. The plank he jumped onto spun, around to try and tip him into the water but, because he had only been on it for a second or two, it failed. Thomas went flying through the air like a long jumper using all his limbs to push himself further through the air. He wasn't going to make it with his feet so he stretched his body out so that he landed on his stomach. Scrambling, with his hands, he tried to pull himself up onto the bank. His legs were trailing in the water. Kicking away, trying to push himself to safety but the more he struggled the more the water resisted. It was as if the water was grabbing hold of his legs and trying to pull him back to drown him in it's murky depths.

"Come on Thomas!" shouted Sam

"Yes, pull harder Thomas!" screamed Rebecca. Topo, however was jumping up and down shouting.

"We'ves gots hims, we'ves gots hims, his nots going to make it's!" She was right. Thomas was losing his battle and was falling back into the water.

"No!" screeched Rebecca panic in her voice. Sam was considering trying to run across the floats to try and help but without the compass he new he would not make it. Topo was still bouncing up and down shouting, "He's not goings to make it's, Alex!" Georgie looked at the mouse then at Thomas and said to herself

'Oh I'm fed up with this.' She raised her arm, wizzer in hand and threw it as hard as she could at Topo, hitting the mouse in the chest. It sent Topo flying backwards into a bush where she disappeared from sight. At once the water around Thomas's feet gave way and he crawled out onto the bank. Rebecca, Sam and Georgie let out a huge cheer and Thomas jumped up and down, his hands above his head.

"I knew it!" exclaimed Georgie. "The more that mouse got excited, the harder the water tried to stop Thomas." She caught her returning wizzer in her hand and looked rather pleased with herself.

"Thanks Georgie!" shouted Thomas from across the water.

"No! That is definitely cheating and you will......" Alex didn't finish his sentence. He had started to move toward Georgie, with an evil look on his huge face. Sam had seen this and decided to act. He threw his stone and hit Alex on the side of the head. The stone returned to Sam and he caught it. For a few seconds Alex stood motionless then his knees buckled and he fell face first into the dirt.

"Right that's them dealt with. "Sam said triumphantly.

"Thomas find the lever," shouted Rebecca. She needn't have bothered. Thomas was already looking and had found it quite quickly. He pulled the lever down and the fire in the tunnel entrance went out. Now their route was clear and Thomas was making his way back across the water.

"We had better hurry!" shouted Georgie, pointing down the road that they had come along earlier. Sam and Rebecca followed Goergie's gaze. They were looking at ten or twelve large teddies, dressed as policeman, running in their direction.

"Come on Thomas, we've got to go!" shouted Sam. Georgie and Rebecca were already making there way to the tunnel. Sam and Thomas were soon following them. They had a good start on the teddies so had time to think. Once inside, light began to come from the walls, as in the tunnels before.

"How are we going to stop them following." asked Georgie in an anxious tone?

"Try that." said Rebecca pointing to a lever on the tunnel wall.

"Well done Rebecca" said Sam. Thomas grabbed the lever and pulled with all his strength but he couldn't move it so Sam had to help.

"Hurry up boys!" shouted the girls as the teddies were getting very close to the entrance.

"Pull Sam!" yelled Thomas and together they did it. The lever moved and the fire reappeared in the tunnel entrance, blocking the route of the teddy policemen. The children all gave a sigh of relief as they realised they were safe once more (well for a little at least).

Chapter Twelve

The Question Master

This tunnel was very short, no more than two or three hundred yards long. Unfortunately they had left their backpacks at the water's edge. This was where they had put them while Thomas was completing the trial. There had been no time to retrieve them before darting into the tunnel. However they were not worried as Alex The Bear had told them they were very nearly home. They came out into a dark, damp, circular chamber. There were no other tunnels, just a staircase rising up around the wall. They could not see the top but it was obvious that the next stage of their journey was upwards.

"There's no point in stopping here." remarked Thomas. "We may as well start climbing right away."

"Sounds good to me." replied Sam and he was first onto the staircase. The steps were only wide enough for the children to go single file so Sam went first Rebecca followed him, Georgie came next, with Thomas bringing up the rear. It was a hard climb. Some of the steps were very shaky so they had to be very careful not to fall. Also the higher they went the further down they had to fall and the view over the edge was very frightening to the children. It did make them feel better to be going upwards though. For the first time in days they felt like they really were on their way home. It took them two hours to complete the climb and they were all totally fed up by the time Sam turned to say,

"We've made it."

"What can you see?" asked Thomas from the back.

"There's a big black door" Sam replied.

"Can you open it Sam?" asked Georgie.

"Give me a chance and I'll try." he snapped and stepped up to the door.

"Let me help." said Rebecca, despite being worried about what might be on the other side of the door. They had to push the door open but it was hard work so Georgie and Thomas helped. Soon the door gave way and they all fell through, landing in a heap on a grey stone floor. Once again they were in a chamber. This one was small, warm and well lit by torches on the walls. On the other side of the chamber was another door and in the middle of the room was a dais. On the dais was a high backed red and gold chair like some kind of throne. Upon the chair sat what looked like an old woman in torn and dusty robes, holding a long wooden staff. The figure appeared to be asleep and on it's shoulder sat a small silver bird. The children regarded the sleeping figure then Georgie whispered.

"Come on. Let's see if we can sneak past and get through the next door without waking her."

"Who said it was a lady?" asked Sam.

"No one but it's obvious Isn't it?" chirped Rebecca.

"Oh stop arguing and let's get moving." put in Thomas. So they all got to their feet, treading very carefully towards the dais and the other door. As they became level with the dais, the figure spoke.

"The door is locked. Only I can open it. Come stand in front of me." it demanded. The figure had not moved but from the voice they could tell Rebecca had been right. It was female. The children moved to stand in front of the figure as they had been told to do. She raised her head, looked at all four and smiled. "Welcome. I am The Question Master." she said. "To return to your world you must all answer a question that I will ask you. Only then may you pass through the door behind me." She took a deep breath and stared at all the children in turn. Finally Rebecca asked

"Will the door take us home?"

"It will return you to the world above; the human world." answered The Question Master.

"What happens if we answer the question wrong?" inquired Sam in a rather worried tone.

"Then you have to take my place. It's the only way I can leave. Someone always has to sit upon this chair. It will then be up to you to ask a question of anyone who enters this chamber. If they answer incorrectly then you may leave and so on. Now, before we start, tell me your names."

"I'm Georgie, this is Rebecca,"

" I'm Thomas and this is Sam."

"Very good, now we may begin" said The Question Master.

"I'm sorry to interrupt but is your name Dorothy?" asked Thomas in a rush. The Question Master regarded Thomas for a moment and looked like she might explode. Eventually she answered

"Yes, I am, or at least I was called Dorothy until the day I entered this room but how did you know my name?"

Tintonia

"We met someone called Professor Mckintey and a Dr Hitzvelgar. They told us about other human children who had tried to return home." said Rebecca.

"Also you wrote your name on the wall of a tunnel." added Georgie.

"So I did, I remember now" said The Question Master.

"We were told you had a silver bird like the one on your shoulder as well." chipped in Sam.

"So I suppose we all just guessed it was you." finished Thomas.

"Mckintey and Hitzvelgar still alive?" mumbled The Question Master to herself more than anyone else. "Oh bliss. What wonderful news, I thought they would all be prisoners of the dwarfs by now." She continued in a more excited tone. "Helga, my best friend was captured you know? She fell from her horse. There was nothing that I could do to save her." She stopped for a moment and all was very quiet. After a while she spoke again. "I wonder what happened to her? she asked herself as if the children were not there then, "There was a boy called Joseph. Do you have news of him? she asked urgently.

"Joseph met his end in the Giant's bone field. Rebecca and I found his bones. We were told that Helga died in the Dwarf mines. I'm very sorry you must miss them terribly" said Georgie.

"Yes I do. It gets very lonely here." whispered The Question Master sadly.

"Well, that's you two home!" Exclaimed Sam in a triumphant voice pointing at Thomas and Georgie.

"What do you mean boy?" asked The Question Master, no longer whispering.

"You asked Thomas how he knew your name and Georgie about Helga and Joseph. They both answered truthfully and correctly, so surely they can pass through the door?" Sam said all this in a matter of fact kind of way, but didn't like the expression on The Question Master's face at all. Then with a crack and a squeak the door behind her opened. She looked around, then back to the children and hissed,

"You two may pass." So Thomas and Georgie started to walk toward the door. Georgie looked to The Question Master and asked her

"Can we stay?"

"No. Once someone has answered a question, they must leave this room. You must wait on the other side." So Thomas and Georgie had to walk through the door and leave Sam and Rebecca to their fate. "Now, for you two." growled The Question Master, looking down her nose at Sam and Rebecca. "You tricked me before, but it won't happen again. You!" she said spinning to face Rebecca pointing, her staff at her.

"Yes," muttered Rebecca in a very squeaky frightened voice. Sam put his hand on her shoulder to reassure her saying,

"Don't worry Becks, you can do it."

"Don't be so sure." hissed The Question Master once again. She looked at Rebecca with steely eyes and asked. "What do you call a baby giraffe?" The question quite took Rebecca by surprise, even though she knew one was coming. Then a wry smile began to form on her pretty little face.

"Come on Becks, think hard" urged Sam.

"Be quiet!" barked The Question Master. "Do not interfere. She must answer on her own." Rebecca looked at Sam and said

"It's O.K. I know the answer. Kevin told me once. Now what was it. Let me think. Oh yes I remember." Her first thought had been a foal but somehow she knew that was wrong. Then it came to her "A calf!" she yelled "A calf. It's a calf."

"Correct." was all The Question Master said in a strangled tone and the door swung open once again. Rebecca walked through, leaving Sam all alone. She wished him luck before she went and had given him a hug to try to make him feel better. But the look on Sam's face was one of complete horror. He wasn't used to girlie displays of affection. The Question Master now looked to Sam; her eyes cold and unforgiving. Sam was trying to be brave and not show his fear but inside he was very frightened. He was on his own and not sure that he could answer a question like 'What do you call a baby giraffe.' He looked to The Question Master's face again and saw that her expression had changed. She now wore a kind look, warm and forgiving, not cold and horrid as before. Sam was sure he could even see a tear on her cheek.

"No one has called me Dorothy for so many years." she mumbled to herself. "I had almost forgotten who I was and like you how frightened when I stood where you now stand. I wish we had all stayed together, just like, you Rebecca, Georgie and Thomas. There is strength in togetherness. You can support each other. Never forget that Samuel." Again she looked him straight in the eye and again he could see the change in her face. "Now I must ask you a question. Mmm let me see. Oh yes, I know. What is your favourite colour?" Sam just looked puzzled as if the question was too hard. He just hadn't expected anything like that. He thought The Question Master must be trying to trick him. "It is not a trick question." she said, as if reading his mind. "Just tell me your favorite colour."

"Green!" blurted out Sam "Green!" The door swung open again and Sam looked at it amazed at his good fortune. He turned to Dorothy, who was now in tears, on her throne and asked "Why such an easy question?" She raised her head and answered

"Because I could not bear to separate you from your companions, how could I have faced them on the other side of that door?"

"Thank you." said Sam, then he had an idea. "Why don't you come with me?"

"I cannot. As I have already said, someone must always sit on this throne, or no one may pass through the door in the future. Thank you for thinking of me though, now go and join the others. They will be worried." So Sam ran through the door to find the others waiting for him on the other side.

Chapter Thirteen

Back To The World Above

It was a rather overcast day in Helston. For those of you who don't know, Helston is a town in Cornwall. The main street is on a hill and at the bottom of the hill there is a bowling green. You can walk on down from the bowling green to the old cattle market and into the park with it's boating lake. Walk further into the park and you will find a thicket of trees and bushes running along a bank. This is where we find Thomas, Rebecca and Georgie. It is also where we pick up our story. Although some way from the boating lake, they could still hear the sounds of children playing and the traffic out on the road. All three however were in a state of intense concentration, with anticipation all over their faces. They were waiting for Sam and were beginning to wonder if he was ever going to join them. Then, as if by magic (which of course it was) the foliage in front of them parted. A hole appeared in the bank and Sam came tumbling out onto the ground in front of them. Then the hole closed, the foliage drew back across the gap and all was normal again. Thomas, Rebecca and Georgie rushed up to Sam and helped him to his feet. They quizzed him about what had happened with The Question Master after Rebecca had passed through the door and he told them everything eagerly. The next problem was to work out where they were.

"Well, one thing's for sure. This isn't where we went into Tintonia" Georgie said.

"No, that's not our lake and there's no rope swing." said Rebecca.

"It is very familiar, though" Sam pointed out.

"I was just thinking the same thing." added Thomas.

"Great minds think alike, eh bro?" Sam joked. They walked around the boating lake and on past the old cattle market, then up past the bowling green and on into the town. They walked up the high street which had a banner across it proclaiming, 'HELSTON WINS MAJOR EUROPEAN HOLIDAY AWARD'

"Helston!" said Georgie surprised "Isn't that in Cornwall?"

"Yes, we've all been there with Kevin and Mum." said Rebecca excitedly.

"But how did we get there this time?" asked Sam.

"It doesn't matter right now. Our problem now is how we get home?" said Thomas.

"Mum has always told us, that if we are lost we should find a policeman or someone in uniform" Rebecca offered wisely.

"That's a good idea, Rebecca," said Sam "but I can't see anyone like that around." They had been steadily walking up the high street and were now at the top on a sort of staggered cross roads. There they found a telephone box.

"I think the best thing to do would be to ring Mum and Kevin first. They can organise for the police to pick us up if they want to." Thomas said, as if trying to convince himself.

"O.K. but you had better be careful what you say Thomas. Remember we've been gone for over a week." Sam warned him.

"Hey, who said I was going to make the call?" Thomas said angrily.

"It was your idea to call." Georgie reminded him.

"That's right, it was your idea." insisted Rebecca.

Tintonia

"O.K. O.K. I think I still have some coins in my bag with the compass. I don't know why but I've been hanging on to them." So Thomas went into the telephone box took a deep breath and called home.

Thomas and Rebecca's Mum, Jane and Sam and Georgie's Father, Kevin had bought new dining room curtains and were in the process of hanging them when the telephone began to ring in the hallway.

"Will you get that please? I want to finish the hooks on this other curtain." Jane asked Kevin.

"O.K. no problem." said Kevin and off he went out into the hallway and picked up the telephone. "Hello. Can I help?" he asked in his best telephone voice.

"Hello Kevin, it's Thomas." Came the reply.

"Thomas, what are you doing on the phone? Why aren't you at the lake?"

"We were" answered Thomas. "But now we're in Helston, in Cornwall. Did you miss us." There was a short silence, while Kevin checked the time by the hall clock, then he said.

"Thomas, I don't know who has put you up to this but you have only been gone for forty-five minutes, so how could you possibly be in Cornwall?"

"Forty five minutes? But we thought we had been gone for a week or more." came Thomas's reply.

"No, forty five minutes, so where are you now and why didn't you stay by the lake as you had been told to do?" Kevin was now starting to sound rather annoyed. Also Jane, having overheard some of the conversation, had come out into the hallway to find out what was going on.

"I've told you." Thomas answered, frustration in his voice "we're in Cornwall, in Helston and we thought we had been gone for a week."

"Put Georgie on the phone!" barked Kevin, rather harshly.

"Hi Dad. We've had a great adventure and I met a real prince!"

"Never mind all that!" Interrupted Kevin. "Where on Earth are you?"

"In Helston, in Cornwall just like Thomas said." answered Georgie.

"You can't be in Cornwall." Kevin started to argue but Georgie interrupted saying,

"Sorry Dad. The money's running out. Let me give you the number so that you can call us back." Georgie gave Kevin the telephone number then the line went dead. Kevin turned to Jane and tried to explain the conversation he had just had with Thomas and Georgie.

"But they can't be in Cornwall" insisted Jane thinking that Kevin must have got the story all wrong.

"Well that's what they said, Helston in Cornwall. Look this is the telephone number Georgie gave me and it's not local." Jane looked at the number and said

"I'm sure this is a Cornwall number." Jane is herself from Cornwall and recognised the code as one she used to call family there from time to time. They stared at each other for a while then Kevin said,

"You call them back and I will go to check the lake to see if they're messing around." He then left in a hurry. The children had been waiting patiently and while they waited Thomas and Georgie relayed the conversation with Kevin to Sam and Rebecca; especially the bit about only having been gone for forty five minutes.

"That must be why Hitzvelgar and Mckinty haven't aged or grown like they would have in our world." said Thomas. "It's the time difference.

"So even though we think we have been away for days, it's actually the same day that we left?" moaned Sam.

"That's about it." confirmed Georgie.

"Oh no, so we haven't missed any school after all." moaned Rebecca. With that, the telephone rang and Thomas answered it.

"Hello Mum. Listen we're not lying. We really are in Cornwall and we really have been on an adventure."

"Thomas, if this some kind of prank please say so now and no one will be in trouble." was Jane's reply. Jane could hear Thomas say to the others,

"She doesn't believe me." and then Sam say,

"Hold on, I have an idea." Jane couldn't see but Sam went up to a lady in the street and asked.

"Could you please come and talk to the lady on the phone and tell her where we are? She doesn't believe us." The next voice Jane heard was a thickly Cornish one. She had a brief conversation with the lady and then asked to be handed back to Thomas.

"You see Mum, we really are in Cornwall." pleaded Thomas.

"It would seem so. I don't know how you managed it but it would appear to be true. Now listen to me, stay by the phone and I will call back and let you know what to do next." As Jane put the telephone down Kevin returned, having checked by the lake and having found no site of the children. Jane explained about the conversations with Thomas and the lady who had been called Mrs Samson. She told Kevin that, however silly it seemed, she thought that the children must be in Cornwall after all.

"If that's the case, what are we going to do?" Kevin asked Jane.

"I will ring Mum and Dad and ask them to collect the children. we can travel down overnight." Kevin agreed and went to get ready for the trip. Jane called her parents who live in Cornwall in a place called Mousehole, near Penzance not far from Helston. She gave them a brief account of what had happened and asked them to collect the children. They agreed without any fuss and set off for Helston at once. Jane then called the children in Helston and told them to wait by the bowling green, for their Grandparents. By that time Kevin had packed a bag so they jumped in the car and headed for Cornwall. The children made their way back down the high street to the bowling green, picking up crisps, cakes and drinks on the way with what money they had left. They had a little picnic while they waited.

Chapter Fourteen

How, Why, Where And When

Jane's parents are called John and Elizabeth and they were a little confused and concerned by what Jane had told them on the telephone. They drove to Helston all the same, not really believing that they would find the children there at all. So imagine their surprise when all four came running up to the car, all excited with stories of giants and dwarfs.

"Alright calm down all of you." said John. "Liz, you call Jane on the mobile and let her and Kevin know that everyone's safe and well." So, on the way to Mousehole, the children sat in the car and listened to Thomas and

Rebecca's Grandparents talking to Jane and Kevin on the mobile. When they had finished Thomas asked,

"Can we tell you about our adventure now Nanny?"

"Not yet." she replied. "Wait until we get home and we can sit down with a nice cup of tea and listen to you all properly. I don't want to miss anything." So later that same day all four children were seated at the dining room table with Janes' parents, telling the whole story from start to finish. Liz, Jane's mother used to be a school-teacher so she knew how to get everything out of the children and how to quiz them about all the relevant facts. They talked for hours while John made drinks and sandwiches for everyone. When the story was finished, Liz stood and said.

"Well that was an interesting adventure you have all had. I am glad that you had the good sense to phone home just as soon as you could. Now, all of you, off to bed because it's late and you have a long journey ahead of you tomorrow and this time a very boring one, by road."

"You do believe us, don't you?" said Rebecca.

"Of course I do, Now off you go and don't forget to wash first." The children didn't argue as they were to tired and they were soon tucked up, in bed fast asleep. When the children were finally settled, John and Liz sat at the table examining the compass, wizzer and Sam's stone.

"You don't seriously believe all this nonsense do you Liz?" demanded John.

"Of course. Don't you?" answered Liz.

"But it can't be true."

"How do you explain all this then" said Liz pointing to the table.

"But this is just a piece of wood in a leather bag. They say it's a compass but it has no face or pointer."

"They told you it will only work for Thomas and only in Tintonia. Weren't you listening, John?"

"But this is just an old stone and this Wizzer thing is supposed to be some sort of Boomerang but it doesn't look anything like one."

"To you, maybe but to them they are something quite different. As they have said they only work in Tintonia, Have faith. I certainly didn't think they were lying, did you?"

"Well no, I agree they did sound very convincing but you can't really believe that they have been in another world Liz?"

"Why not? How do you explain how they got to Cornwall in forty five-minuets? Surely you're not suggesting that Jane and Kevin are lying to us about that are you?"

"No, no not at all. It's just a very unbelievable story that's all." There was a long silence while they finished their tea, then Liz said,

"What was it that Sherlock Holmes used to say? When you have eliminated all of the possible solutions then whatever is left must be the answer, however impossible that may seem. Well something like that anyway!" With that they went to bed and slept with visions of giants and goblins in their dreams, just like the children. In the morning Jane and Kevin arrived so the children had to go through the whole process again. Not that they didn't enjoy that of course. They were bursting to tell anyone who would listen. Kevin and Jane listened intently. They asked questions without sounding too patronising and reassured the children they were not in trouble. After all, they had all stuck together and had helped each other through a difficult time. The whole thing could have been dismissed had it not been for the time difference. As nothing else could be proved or disproved, the adults decided to let the children think that they had believed them. However, the children were told not to tell anyone outside of the family about the adventure, as they might get teased or be thought strange; maybe even mad. Jane and Kevin also decided to stay on in Cornwall for a while so the children did miss some school. Once at home and back into their routine, everything soon settled down. After a while the adventure was hardly ever mentioned. Kevin and Jane didn't tell the children that they had checked the history of the house. They had found that some forty years before five other children had gone missing whilst playing by the lake. Dorothy Parkin, her brother Joseph, a friend Ewen Mckinty and their German cousins, Fredric and Helga Hizvelgar. A Mr and Mrs Parkin had owned the house and there had been a terrible fuss at the time but the children had never been found.

Chapter Fifteen

The Beginning Of The End Or The End Of The Beginning

Some time passed, perhaps almost a year before the children were allowed to roam once again. They kept close to the house at first but gradually ventured further. One of the first things they did however was to check out the spot were Georgie had fallen into the earth but everything was normal. One day they were skimming stones across the lake and taking turns on the rope swing just as they had been all that time before, when a voice from behind them drew their attention. "Oh, thank God I've found you all.

Kevin Gritten

It's taken me ages." There was a figure, leant up against a tree. He started to sob. Georgie and Rebecca just stood opened mouthed in utter amazement. Sam and Thomas both shouted together "Gordo!" All four children ran to their friend to help.

"How did you get here Gordo?" asked Thomas.

"Why is your arm bleeding?" said Georgie.

"Please don't cry" pleaded Rebecca.

"I don't suppose you have any of that Elfin beer with you Gordo?" was all Sam could manage. The other three just glared at Sam in disgust so looking a bit sheepish he added "What's the matter Gordo?"

"What's the matter? What's the matter? I'll tell you what the matter is. The dwarfs have raided Tintonia. Prince Rodric and Tig Tig have been taken prisoner, along with most of the population. They have taken everything and Tintonia is ablaze. I need your help. You've got to come with me to help rescue them!" The children were speechless. Not one of them knew what to say. Were there adventures about to begin again? Who can say but that's a story for another day.

The End, Possibly....

Printed in the United Kingdom
by Lightning Source UK Ltd.
129347UK00001B/36/A